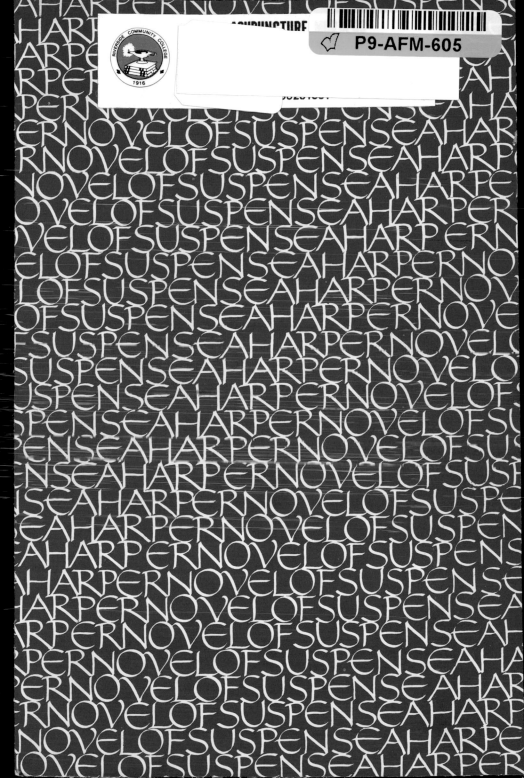

THE
ACUPUNCTURE
MURDERS

THE
ACUPUNCTURE
MURDERS

Dwight Steward

HARPER & ROW, PUBLISHERS
New York Evanston San Francisco London

unae ex partibus
compluribus dedicatur

B.G.S.

A JOAN KAHN-HARPER NOVEL OF SUSPENSE

FIRST EDITION

Designed by Patricia Dunbar

Library of Congress Cataloging in Publication Data

Steward, Dwight.
   The acupuncture murders.
   "A Joan Kahn-Harper novel of suspense."
   I. Title.
PZ4.S8492Ac [PS3569.T459]   813′ .5′4   72-9120
ISBN 0-06-014122-0

For the Reader

A few words of explanation before entering the world of the deaf.

Consider the much misunderstood subject of lip-reading—more accurately called speech-reading, since the movements of the tongue and teeth are also read. The sad fact is that only one-third of the movements required to produce human speech are visible. The rest remain hidden in the mouth or throat. But even if all speech were visible, the deaf person's problems would not be solved. During normal conversation, the articulation of words requires from twelve to twenty movements per second. The human eye, however, can record only eight or nine such movements per second. It is also necessary to remember that most hearing persons, unaware of or indifferent to the plight of the deaf person, do not articulate their words distinctly. For these reasons, a deaf person might speech-read:

"buiuujussaytha"

It is only his acute perception of the situation in which these sounds were spoken which allows him to understand:

"But didn't you just say that?"

In addition, the deaf person must cope with the similarity of articulative movements between sounds which are quite distinct and never confused by hearing persons. The movements producing the sounds of "f" and "ch" are examples. Hence, a person's name, Fletcher, would be seen as:

F/CH? let F/CH? er

To spare the reader the difficulties of such "translation," most of the dialogue in the following account, although told from the point of view of a deaf person, has been normalized.

Finally, the verb "sign" is used frequently in this account to indicate one method of deaf communication. It should be read as the equivalent of "said." The practice of "signing" involves a combination of finger-alphabet spelling, signals which represent complete words or concepts, and improvisation by the signer. It is through the latter especially that the signer supplies the nuances of meaning normally conveyed by a speaker's tempo, tone, and inflection.

THE
ACUPUNCTURE
MURDERS

Introducing

TREHUNE, Sampson. Book appraiser. b. Oyster Bay, L.I., N.Y., April 2, 1929. Son of Richard Ainsworth and (Dame) Cecilia Heatherton Trehune (divorced). M.A. (Honors) Magdalene College, Cambridge, 1954. Conslt. to UNESCO, Paris, 1958–59; fellow, Hispanic Foundation, 1961; ed., *Volta Review*, 1962; spec. conslt., Lib. of Cong., 1966; lect., Cambridge, 1968; bd. of dirs., Nat. Thtr. for the Deaf, 1969–

Author: *Seventeenth-Century American Holographs: A Descriptive Bibliography*, 1958; *A Concise History of Printing in America*, 1966; *A. A. Milne and Winnie the Pooh: Textual Variants*, 1967; numerous articles on the collection and preservation of books. Film (with Nat. Ed. TV): *Shakespeare for the Deaf*, 1970.

Organizations: Am. Antiquarian Soc.; Am. Hearing Soc.; AHA; ALA; Appraisers Internationale; H.E.A.R.; MLA; Nat. Inst. for the Deaf (London); Volta.

Clubs: Grollier (London); Cosmos (Wash.); Cambridge Colonials (N.Y.).

Addresses:

444 W. 29th St., New York, 10017.
14 Hampton Court, London, SW 7.
Heatherton Lane, New Surrey, England (summer).

Honors: LL.D. Amherst, 1968; member, Utek Indian tribe; pres., Bookmen; Scolaire avec palmes; J. B. Hugo Medallion, 1969; Dedicatory Volume No. 4, OXON lectures in bibliography.

Hobbies: the works of A. A. Milne, silent films, the theater.

Special interest: MURDER.

ONE

"Fuck Freud!" Sampson dismissed the Viennese patriarch with a broad wave of his arm, dashes of cocktail sauce marching down Mon Maison's finest white linen. He ate the last oyster off its shell, and noticed the eyes opposite his were smiling.

Damn. He had forgotten to "remember" his voice. After more than thirty years of total deafness, speaking required intense concentration if he were to produce sounds which by any stretch of the imagination could be recognized as human. When he forgot to "remember" it, he was told by various Hearers that his voice was "just too strange to believe," "unearthly," "shocking!" He also had no control over the volume of it. He wondered if anyone else in Mon Maison's dining room had heard him. Or, worse, understood. Raising his napkin to his lips, he glanced around the baroque paneled room. Heads nearly touched at surrounding tables. Lips were twisted in surprise or smirks. Two tables away, an attractive redhead blushed a complementary pink as their eyes met briefly.

Sampson grimaced at his companion, Dr. Robert Abel, and, reading the expression on Abel's face, knew that someone stood behind him, on his right side. Turning, Sampson confronted an expanse of maroon dinner jacket topped by the anxious face of Louis, Mon Maison's ever-hovering maître d'.

("Say 'Luuu-eee,' Mr. Trehune, with the lips so. 'Luuu-eee.'"
Of course, Sampson never succeeded.) Luuu-eee nodded. And
smiled. Abel said something which Sampson did not see. Now
Abel was smiling, too. To hell with them.

Sampson scrunched his thickening frame down into the
plush comfort of Mon Maison's Luuu-eee XIV chairs and
closed his eyes. He could at least be alone. "Oh, Bear of Little
Brain," he began reciting to himself. Vibrations swirled about
him, on both sides and behind. Twice someone brushed his
left arm. When the vibrations ceased, he opened his eyes. The
remains of the oysters and their ice bed had disappeared, replaced by two enormous steaming bowls. The spots of cocktail sauce had been tactfully wiped away. The other patrons,
feeling cheated of a promising spectacle, had grudgingly retreated into their own noisy worlds.

Abel spoke very slowly, as if to a child. "Now, Sampson,
I was merely going to remind you that many of the cures
attributed to acupuncture may in fact be due to the psycho-
somatic nature of the particular—" Sampson shook his head
violently, cutting off Abel, who was exasperated but un-
deterred. "But you must realize that cases of hysterical deafness are not uncommon."

Impatient, Sampson signed, "I may be deaf, but I am not
insane. I am not DUMB." Hysteria could hardly account for
over thirty years of profound deafness; at least, not his. He
had signed the last word boldly, with the gestures of a bom-
bastic actor. Now he noticed that people were staring at him
again. Damn! Abel mouthed on, but Sampson silenced him
by lowering his eyes to the bowl in front of him and hungrily
spooning a chunk of mullet. He raised his eyes to discover
his friend still staring at him. "If God is truly just," spoke Abel
distinctly, "you will find a bone in your bouillabaisse."

After *endive Belge* with the dressing of the house, Abel
surrendered and called for coffee. Sampson loosened his belt

2

a notch, read the dessert menu with exaggerated care, and finally ordered his favorite: a dish which took twenty-five minutes to prepare. Abel fidgeted. "Patience is the supreme virtue, not so?" Sampson signed. The time passed slowly with some small talk.

Finally, the waiter placed a plate in front of Sampson. On it was a quivering molded rectangle, drenched in a caramel-colored sauce. Sampson beamed, then spelled out in the finger alphabet, slowly, as if to a child, "m-o-u-s-s-e s-a-b-a-y-o-n." Then deftly, his two hands moving in quick circles, he signed, "Admire, you Goth! Magnificent! Should stand! Salute! Sing!" Again he resorted to the finger alphabet: "A-l-l-o-n-s e-n-f-a-n-t-s d-e l-a p-a-t-r"—at which point Abel reached across the table and gently slapped Sampson's hand, silencing him in mid-word.

"You're eating so much because you're nervous. You're not sure you want to be treated by acupuncture, but you've committed yourself and can't refuse without losing face. Especially with yourself. Voisin noted that this is far from an unusual reaction in Western patients. In many cases, just the sight of the needles induces hysteria and prevents treatment."

Sampson replied with a one-finger gesture which he had certainly not learned from Stoates's *Manual of Deaf-Mute Signs,* and stabbed the mousse with his fork on the lower right corner. "Point 12, the stomach meridian," an acupuncture chart would read. He swallowed and closed his eyes, savoring the sherry bouquet. Finishing the last speck of the mousse, Sampson dawdled over his coffee and brandy, enjoying the comfortable sensation of a superb meal. Finally, however, the glances of their waiter were becoming palpable to him; they were the last of the luncheon guests. He signaled for the check.

He allowed Abel to outfumble him and scrawled in large

letters across the bill, "SAMPSON TREHUNE." Remembering his expostulation on Freud, he added a far too generous tip.

The two left Mon Maison and strolled leisurely along Ninth Avenue. Sampson belched contentedly and contemplated the evening ahead. Three hours of silent films at the Ciné-Juré and with any luck he might persuade Abel to stay for a second showing. Chaplin, Sennett, and Fields: ecstasy.

His reverie was interrupted by Abel, who faced him with the sort of sad, forlorn expression in his eyes which meant something was amiss. "About tonight, I've got an errand to run. I'm sorry, but I'll have to beg off." Sampson scowled, said nothing. His friend hadn't mentioned any errand before. What could it be at four o'clock on a Saturday afternoon? Some loony? Sampson shrugged his shoulders. So be it.

"Tomorrow," Abel continued, "at eleven. Grand Central and I'll get the tickets, since you picked up lunch today." Sampson nodded impatiently. "I'll meet you outside the gate. There's only one train for Connecticut." He reverted to the doctor. "Don't stay out too late; you need plenty of rest. And remember, don't take any pills—not even aspirin. Voisin will not treat anyone who has ingested drugs of any sort during the twenty-four hours . . ."

And he's off! Breaking well from the gate. Condescending bastard. Why are all doctors like that? Abel rounded the quarter pole, not noticing that Sampson looked his way only occasionally. Instead, Sampson watched the traffic snarled at the corner; then, at the halfway mark, he composed a pseudo *Who's Who* entry: "VOISIN, HENRI; a leading acupuncturist in the Western world; member of the Société Internationale d'acuponcture; equally at home in Western and Eastern medicine; fourteen years in the People's Republic of China, studying and working with needles; lecturer, University of Kiosa, Japan; author of *Acuponcture aujourd'hui*, best-seller in six languages, first English edition published eight months

4

ago." Sampson had read that volume as well as every other one he could find on the subject.

Voisin was the first Western physician to claim a positive cure for nerve deafness by acupuncture. "A simple motion with the needle, so! Insert. Twist. Stimulate. Withdraw, and *voilà!* Hearing returns." Tomorrow, Sampson would find out. Abel moved into the stretch: more advice, having forgotten that Sampson was responsible for securing every book on acupuncture in the doctor's extensive collection, and had read each one before turning it over to him. Even going so far as to slit the uncut pages on a first edition of Soulie de Morant's *Précis de la Vraie Acuponcture Chinoise,* Paris, 1935. This reduced the value of the volume, but Abel would have to cut them anyway, reasoned Sampson, and I do a better job. As a matter of fact, Robert Abel, M.D., still owed Sampson $435 for past purchases. The loonies aren't paying promptly; maybe they're not so loony after all, Sampson thought.

"Till tomorrow, then," Abel said, apparently assured he had won, and moved off to the winner's circle. Sampson tapped him on the shoulder as he turned and spelled "A-u r-e-v-o-i-r m-o-n c-a-p-i-t-a-i-n-e." His movements a parody of Douglas Fairbanks at his worst, he signed, "We who are about to get stuck, salute you!" He jerked his hand to a snappy military salute and marched off, leaving the good doctor muttering to himself.

The walk back to the apartment had left him tired and depressed. Opening the door, he was greeted by an exuberant, if not frantic, schnauzer. Cooped up since early morning, Savvy was desperate. Sampson clipped the leash to the ornate collar that read: "SAVONAROLA MONTESQUIEU CAESAR BORGIA STUBBS/444 W. 29th St., Apt. 2/$200 reward, no questions." Dutifully, he escorted Savvy along the curb to the end of the block and back.

5

Home again, he thought for the hundredth time about the bother of owning a dog. But the salt-and-pepper animal happily gyrating at his feet was such an obvious contrast to his own rather dour mood that he forgot the bother quickly.

Then there was the Dürer. As the last male of the Trehunes, Sampson had unwanted visits from his relatives, who felt sorry for poor "Sampsy" and wished to see him married to carry on the "long Trehune line." "Not that long," Sampson would mumble, pick up Savvy, and stand next to a large painting on his stark white living-room wall. It was an oil copy of an Albrecht Dürer, executed in 1492, and contained the first pictorial representation of the schnauzer breed. Savvy's color and configuration were identical to those of the painted schnauzer. "Now, there, that's breeding—that's a long line," he would say in his worst voice, stroking the dog in his arms.

When in a Scotch mist, Sampson also delighted in detailing the close resemblance between the schnauzer and an infant which appeared in a woodcut Dürer made a few years later. "Lived in Nuremberg then. 1498. Dog cropped in German style. Could not afford child model. Obvious. Woman holds dog, can't you see?" The woodcut, however, was a ten-by-eighteen-inch masterpiece entitled "Madonna and Child" and the New England sense of humor did not extend to the Christ Child. Visits were fewer.

The trek to the Ciné-Juré seemed too much trouble, so Sampson opted for a quiet evening at home. First he switched on the alarm that protected his windows and doors. Next he unplugged the fifteen-inch rotating fan, connected to his doorbell, which notified him of visitors. Tonight, he decided, he was at home to no one.

To Savvy's delight, he took out an ancient cast-iron kettle and prepared a bowl of popcorn soaked in butter. Flopping into a massive recliner chair, he alternated between stuffing

6

handfuls of popcorn into his mouth and throwing pieces into the most unlikely places, which Savvy nevertheless always managed to reach. This lasted ten minutes. The popcorn was gone, he was bored, and he had a case of heartburn.

Moving the recliner into an upright position, he reached for a remote-control gadget and decided to try television. He played spin-the-dial, watching the conclusion of a sukiyaki space opera, five minutes of rerun animated cartoons, the artificial grimaces of two wrestlers, and a half-hour of depressing reports of dollar crises, shootings, wars, a flood, and something about a young woman in a small French town which he couldn't decipher.

For Sampson, however, as much as he hated it, television was more than a pastime. It was his only source for seeing new words, such as the names of people, places, and new products. The latter were especially important. Sampson had never seen "Saran Wrap" spoken, and when Sadie Gorham, the owner of the building, who lived on the first floor, had casually asked him if he would like to "try a roll of Saran," he thought she was making an obscene suggestion. Fortunately for their continued friendship, he had been too tired to pursue the subject.

Tonight, even the grinning, fatuous faces failed to amuse. His indigestion was getting worse. Stupid popcorn. He dropped two tablets into a glass of water, and as they fizzed, he spoke their name aloud several times. Always good for a laugh, he thought, and swallowed the tingling drink.

He paced. He ignored Savvy. Listlessly, he thumbed through a recent Kraus catalog, ticking off a few of the books to be auctioned. But the Kraus sale was next month. His worry was tomorrow.

Succumbing at last, he picked up his well-worn copy of *Acupuncture Today*, and began to read:

Acupuncture, from the Latin *acus*, needle, and *punctura*, to pierce: it is a strange name for an entire system of medicine, and one we, the Western world, have given it. It is not a particularly good name, for it falls short of what the Chinese system of medical care is.

What is this strange practice of curing illness by sticking the body with needles? It is ancient, for one thing, at least four millennia old, predating by at least 2,000 years any cohesive medical system in the West. It is effective, for another, at least as effective as modern Western medicine and, in some types of illness and disease, much more so. It is also alien to Western medical thought, based on the belief that man and nature exist in harmony, sustained by a universal energy that flows through every form of matter that exists. It gives rise to immediate suspicion from Western doctors, because it treats mind and body as one, and man as healthy only when mind, body, and nature all work in harmony. . . .

Sampson flipped the pages of the book casually, pausing briefly at Chapter Three: "The Energy of the Universe." As always, he smiled while reading this chapter. Not only because of the fanciful descriptions, but also because of the thought that the foundations of all Western medicine might be wrong. A delightful prospect, revenge for the probings of various interns and their damn tuning forks.

There is a form of energy, the Chinese believe and have always believed, called *Ch'i*, that flows through man via a system of ducts or channels, called meridians. This universal energy is the very force of life, and determines man's health. The needles of acupuncture, by insertion into the points along the skin where the meridians surface, change the flow of the universal energy. These meridians connect with the internal organs, thus affecting the condition of the organs. . . .

He shook his head and sighed. After all, he was a grown man and, however delightful, such tales of universal energy were hardly creditable. He paused and frowned at a woodcut, first printed in 1789. It depicted a languishing woman with nine punctures in her bare stomach, arranged neatly in rows of three. He shivered slightly in sympathy. The pages immediately following, however, contained not only drawings but also photographs: photographs of grinning Chinese men, women, and children, all with needles protruding from parts of their bodies. But still grinning and waving their copies of Chairman Mao's *Quotations*. He continued turning the pages until he reached the concluding chapter, a chapter he had virtually memorized: "Acupuncture *Today!*"

The modern Chinese people, in their search for better ways to care for the health of the masses by using intrinsic Chinese medicine—acupuncture—have found many startling uses for the needles. Beginning in 1968, the People's Liberation Army health teams traveled the Chinese countryside, treating children afflicted with polio. Clinics were set up for the treatment of nerve deafness and limb paralysis. Remarkable results—cure rates far above fifty percent in all cases—occurred. Intensive study of acupuncture began. . . .

There it was, documented with names, dates, places in an appendix of nearly fifty pages. Treatment of nerve deafness, cure rate above fifty percent in all cases. Tomorrow.

Unimpressed by the lack of Western-style "scientific" explanation for the needle therapy's effectiveness, the Chinese continued their work with deaf and paralyzed patients. Now, for example, virtually every deaf person in China may receive acupuncture treatment, with a high degree of expectation, depending on his age (for some reason children respond better), of having his hearing restored.

Tomorrow was his turn. He and a man named Wolberg were to be guinea pigs at a secret session held by a few enthusiastic doctors, headed by Dr. Richard Altman, so that they might witness acupuncture treatment for themselves. Conducting this clandestine meeting, at the Altman Clinic, would be Henri Voisin, whose picture now stared back at Sampson from the book's dust jacket.

"What do you have to worry about?" Abel had demanded. "Every doctor attending is risking his career just being there. You and Wolberg, what do you have to lose? Just get stuck by a needle or two. And think of what you have to gain!" It was true. Just a needle or two. He had certainly endured more, much more. "But just don't get your hopes raised too much," Abel had cautioned. Yet the miserable have no other medicine, only hope. With all his psychiatry, Abel might not ever understand that. Nor would he understand Sampson's hesitation. "After all, you do want to be normal again, don't you? To hear again?" Normal! He had seen the Hearers, the normal ones. Seen them shudder on subway platforms as the trains zoomed by. On Times Square, seen them grow visibly wilted, and worse, by the noise of traffic. The eyes of the Hearers, of those who live in a world of alarm clocks, jangling telephones, jackhammers, unceasing noise—those eyes bothered him. Did he really want to hear?

Enough. He closed the book and went determinedly to the kitchen. Large tumbler, lots of ice, to the brim with Scotch. Two glasses and several hours later, Savvy anxiously pulled at his cuff as he slept in the chair. "Sorry, fellow," Sampson mumbled. "Tomorrow."

Just past nine the following morning, fortified by a large breakfast, three Bloody Marys, and firm resolutions, Sampson disturbed Sunday morning's tranquillity by pounding on T.J.'s door. Tough on the Hearers, he thought as he pounded again. T.J. (so dubbed by Sampson, for "timid" and "Jewish") was Sampson's close friend as well as upstairs neighbor. Reluctantly, the door opened and Savvy bounded into the room.

"Up late re-hears-ing," T.J. mouthed, standing at the door in pajamas. He always spoke to Sampson that way: slow-ly, dis-tinct-ly. Maddening! When T.J. first discovered that Sampson was deaf, the two men were standing on the corner of Broadway and Twenty-ninth, and he offered instinctively to help Sampson across the street. Hearers were all alike.

Sampson stared at the bedraggled, almost miniature man. "What is it this time?" he asked, not really caring.

"Lax-a-tives. You have no i-de-a how dif-fi-cult it is to sound sin-cere and sex-y when you are talk-ing a-bout a lax-a-tive." He took almost a full minute to utter the last sentence, Sampson nodding impatiently, having heard the same speech dozens of times before. Despite his far from prepossessing appearance, T.J. was a television star—of sorts. His voice, so Sampson had been assured, just oozed masculinity, and he made a comfortable living doing voice overlays for television and radio commercials. "You hear my voice two, three times a day," he had once bragged.

"I never hear anything," Sampson had corrected, and added suspiciously, "You can make a living talking for thirty seconds every couple of weeks?"

"Re-sid-u-als. It's called re-sid-u-als."

"What's a residual?" Sampson had asked, and a half-hour later wished he hadn't.

Suddenly T.J. disappeared into the bedroom, and just as suddenly Savvy scooted out. Savvy had discovered long ago that barking at Sampson got no response, so he rarely barked at home. But T.J., of course, was a different matter. When Savvy barked, T.J. jumped. Savvy barked a lot when he stayed with T.J.

When T.J. reappeared in his bathrobe, Sampson said, "He's

11

fed. See you," hoping to get away without a long discussion of today's planned treatment.

"Good luck, Sam. I know how much this means. What can I say? Good luck. Any-way, en-joy the trip. Con-nect-i-cut's pret-ty in the fall. I re-mem-ber once—"

"Thanks."

Back in his own apartment, Sampson carefully packed six copies of Voisin's book in his briefcase. The publisher, skeptical, had made a small first printing, and the early books were characterized by a misnumbered page. The book was an instant success, and of course later editions were corrected. Six first editions, autographed by the author, would appreciate considerably in a very short time. Even if he didn't hear autumn winds whispering in the trees, he'd pick up a few dollars. And at times the bills from Mon Maison frightened even him.

He switched on the alarm and, descending the steps, looked back at the door rather wistfully. He had been present when the alarm was installed over a year before by "a friend in the business" recommended by T.J. Curious, Sampson had tested it. Savvy had jumped as though hit by an electric shock, running from room to room, chasing his tail, and finally attacking the electrician. The unfortunate man had moved to turn the alarm off, but Sampson seized his arm, fascinated. The man could barely resist, shaking uncontrollably, his eyes brimming with tears. At last, he jerked free and flicked off the switch.

By Sampson's estimate, the alarm had been active for about thirty seconds. Still shaking, the man had yelled at him, "Buddy, don't you know how loud that thing is?" After a moment, Sampson asked as politely as he could, "What does *loud* mean?"

The man shook his head and yelled something which Sampson couldn't see, jerking the apartment door open. Sadie from downstairs, T.J., and three unknowns were frozen in the halls

12

and on the stairs, looking a little curious and more than a little frightened. Slapping his ears and still quivering a bit, the man said something, pointed at Sampson, and hurried away—returning briefly for his tool case. Sampson waved to the people in the hall, making signs that everything was in order. Closing the door, he had smiled and begun to sing, croakingly, "It's a beautiful house, tiddley-pom," and was unreasonably happy for the rest of the weekend.

Gleefully, he had told Abel, and immediately realized his mistake. "You are unnecessarily bitter and unfair in your reactions to normal people. Obviously, it's just a form of compensation for your own shortcomings. Understandable, perhaps, from a purely clinical point of view, but certainly not to be encouraged by such toys."

"You going to send me a bill?"

"That whole apartment of yours, it's—it's hardly healthy. Why, the way you have it wired, it's like an extension of your personality. You don't feel you are a complete person unless you are 'plugged-in'—Bettelheim's phrase, I believe. Why, it's just like a womb," he insisted, his eyes glazing as he spoke. "Yes, you feel defenseless, exposed, when you are outside its protecting walls. Just like a womb."

Sampson paused for a moment now, and looked up at his windows. Then, feeling rather exposed, he hurried along near-deserted streets on his way to Grand Central. Fuck Freud.

TWO

"If you want to know a man, to tell whether he's lying, for instance," Sampson often pronounced, "don't look at his words, look at his hands."

Henri Voisin was easy to read since, like many of his Gallic compatriots, he almost literally spoke with his hands. Despite his intense gaze and the air of assurance which wafted from him, Voisin was not at all distinguished-looking. The tailoring of his clothes and the style of his haircut were typically European. Moreover, decided Sampson, once more categorizing a person by color, he was gray: gray eyes, thinning gray hair, gray mustache, a gray suit, and even a grayish skin tone. Judging by the current reaction of the Hearers gathered in the Altman Clinic, Voisin's voice was probably gray, too. Only his hands had color—drawing, punctuating, and describing his whole state of mind. A pity such talent was wasted on a Hearer.

Having met him three weeks before at a luncheon arranged by Abel, Sampson did not have to inspect Harrison Wolberg, Voisin's patient, who now faced him from the table. Now, as then, Wolberg was brown: disheveled dark brown hair, light brown eyes, teeth browned by tobacco, and brown suit trousers. The sweat staining his yellow silk shirt was brown-rimmed, too.

During their first meeting, Sampson had been annoyed— unreasonably, he later admitted. Harrison Wolberg had suffered a mild coronary a year earlier, and as a result the right side of his face was paralyzed. Sampson wasn't particularly bothered by the uncontrollable and seemingly lidless right eye which stared at him. But when Wolberg spoke, he hardly moved his lips. Instead, words slid from a sloping gap on the left side of his mouth, owing, naturally, to paralysis of the muscles controlling his lips, tongue, and throat. Sampson strained to understand the man, but it was nearly impossible. Discussing the impending acupuncture treatment they were both to undergo, Wolberg did demonstrate an unexpected sense of humor. "Should get a picture with needles sticking in me; good advertisement for Wolberg Brothers. Can just see it in *Barron's:* 'First human pincushion on the curb.' After all, everyone at one time or another has wanted to stick needles into his stockbroker." The left side of Wolberg's face twisted into a smile and Sampson felt a bond of kinship between the afflicted.

But then Wolberg had begun on the stock market, and had queried Sampson about his portfolio. "It's black, about fourteen by twenty-four, calfskin," Sampson signed to Abel, who slapped his wrist and shook his head at him.

"Mr. Trehune does not feel in a position at this moment to expand his holdings," said Abel. Wolberg nodded but continued, "Should you ever change your mind, look me up. We specialize in new issues and, as you are probably aware, this is a new-issue market. I've got a couple of red herrings on my desk now which are really exciting." He handed Sampson his card. Sampson nodded and left Wolberg and Abel to discuss those particular herrings while he turned his attention to the herrings—filet, in sour cream—which sat before him. They were barely adequate. "Out of a jar," he had signed to Abel. Another reason he remembered the meeting with distaste.

Now Voisin gestured, probably silencing the audience. "I have taken my own pulses already and will be able to compensate for them when I read Mr. Wolberg's. For the benefit of my colleagues who have never witnessed acupuncture treatment, and also for our lovely skeptic . . ." Voisin turned his head and bowed slightly. Sampson missed what followed. In a moment, he picked up the thread again.

"Take the first finger of your right hand, please, and place it so, on your left wrist. You now feel your pulse, yes? That is the superficial pulse. Please, push down, hard. You feel now, perhaps, a slightly different pulse? Good. That is the deep pulse. In acupuncture, the doctor must read both pulses, superficial and deep, six on each wrist. Twelve readings in all—corresponding to each of the twelve major internal organs."

Sampson grew impatient. He had learned of the several pulses long ago and had demonstrated to his own satisfaction on himself, T.J., Sadie, even on Savvy, that despite what Western medicine maintained, there was more than one pulse.

Moving his head and again obscuring the words, Voisin carried on: "Each internal organ expresses itself in subtle characteristics of the pulses . . . along radial artery . . . small intestine, bladder, heart . . . left wrist . . . right wrist, stomach . . . large intestine . . . deep pulse lungs, spleen." For the next fifteen minutes, Sampson watched as Voisin's hands moved along the wrists of Wolberg, the doctor alternating between frowns and nods, sometimes speaking but mostly quiet—almost as though he were listening. As he watched, Sampson discovered a whole new meaning for the medical cliché "laying on hands."

Finally finished, Voisin placed Wolberg's right wrist on the table and smiled proudly, as though he had discovered a holograph of the Old Testament. Gone was the fascinating action of his hands.

"Mr. Wolberg is nervous," Voisin announced grandly. Sampson fumed. Of course he's nervous, you boor. Anyone

16

could see that. He refrained from shouting, and toyed with the idea of leaving at once. "You feel nervous, Mr. Wolberg?" Voisin again. Wolberg nodded nervously. "Aha!" Voisin, triumphant. Sampson croaked a four-letter word of Anglo-Saxon abstraction and looked around at the others. With the exception of a woman, they were all nodding sagely as if they were in the presence of ultimate wisdom suddenly revealed. Sampson muttered another obscenity, questioning the parentage of all doctors, East and West.

Even if it worked for Wolberg, it probably wouldn't work for him. Got to remember: be realistic. I am deaf—never change.

When Sampson looked at Voisin again, he had Wolberg's right wrist resting on his palm and was brandishing a three-inch hairbreadth needle, barely visible. "The problem originated in the large intestine, and so I remove the problem by a simple puncture." Voisin's hand poised for a short count above Wolberg's, then swiftly struck the needle into the web of flesh joining Wolberg's thumb and first finger. Voisin spun the needle slightly between his fingers, and jabbed it a bit deeper. "Does that hurt, Mr. Wolberg?"

The moment Voisin had picked up the needle from the tray held by Altman's nurse, Wolberg had closed his eyes and tightened his jaw, obviously gritting his teeth against the approaching puncture. "No, no, nothing," said Wolberg. "Please, you will lie down, yes?" Wolberg did, and Voisin continued, "A simple procedure. The point is called 'Ho Ku,' and treatment consists of penetration to the depth of ten millimeters and twisting, clockwise." The needle still in place, Voisin began taking Wolberg's pulses. "The needle should be removed when the pulses show there is improvement. Now!" Again with the air of a magician performing a miracle, Voisin removed the needle and, smiling, displayed it to his audience. Did he expect applause?

17

Voisin helped Wolberg to sit up, then turned him to face the audience. Sampson dropped his briefcase—apparently with some noise, since the others looked suddenly in his direction. He was astounded. Even though it was only the end of Act One, Voisin deserved applause. The right side of Wolberg's face, still paralyzed, was, of course, unchanged. But the left! The muscles around the jaw were relaxed. His whole body, his carriage, the way he dropped his hands in his lap, the way he held his neck—several more items which Sampson registered —were different. Either the acupuncture was successful or Harrison Wolberg was dissembling, proving himself the greatest actor ever. In any case, he was no longer the bundle of jangling nerves he had been. Sampson hurriedly picked up his briefcase and stared anxiously at Wolberg. Voisin said something which Sampson didn't see.

"No, no," Wolberg said in answer, shaking his head.

"You feel better?"

"Yes," nodding his head.

"Good, good. Can you find the spot where the needle was inserted?"

Wolberg looked at his hand, again shook his head.

"There is no pain? No blood?"

"No."

"Now we begin."

Deserting Wolberg, Voisin moved to the large chart near the center of the operating room. Gruesome thing, Sampson thought. The body of a human male was outlined on the chart, his mouth turned in sorrow like a mask of tragedy, his body covered with lines in red and countless numbers in blue. Next to the body was printed a larger-than-life human head— a different man, obviously, but also unhappy and also covered with red lines and blue numbers. As Voisin spoke, he emphasized his remarks by pricking the numbered points on the chart with an acupuncture needle—a practice which did nothing to decrease Sampson's returning nervousness.

"Mr. Wolberg has suffered what you call in Western medicine a stroke, resulting in partial paralysis of his right side, most noticeably the muscles of his face, which control his eyelid, lips, tongue, and so forth. These are symptoms which Western physicians would trace to their immediate cause; namely, the heart." Voisin recited almost verbatim from his own book. "For an acupuncturist, however, the true origin of the paralysis lies in a subtle malfunction of one of the twelve basic organs. My diagnosis, confirmed after reading Mr. Wolberg's pulses, traces the cause of the paralysis to his stomach, gall bladder, and Triple Warmer. To treat this pa tient, I shall make a total of twelve punctures along the meridians of these organs."

Voisin jabbed at several points around the face printed on the chart. "Puncture two, gall-bladder meridian, tip of the ear lobe. So. The Triple Warmer, point six, tip of right ear." Sampson's doubts about the worth of acupuncture returned and he sank into his seat, ignoring Voisin. The Triple Warmer! An organ which, according to Western science, simply did not exist. The closest approximation was in the function of several different glands. But, according to acupuncture, the Triple Warmer was responsible for the circulation of nervous energy and warmth throughout the body, including blood and sexual fluids. And for four thousand years the Chinese had been treating patients as though such an organ actually existed—and curing patients by correcting the imbalance in this nonextant organ.

Sampson was drawn from his doubts by movement around him. Voisin, who had returned to Wolberg, was joined by Drs. Abel and Altman. "Since the purpose of this demonstration is to teach as well as to cure, I have asked these two physicians to assist me. I need not stress that although acu-

19

puncture treatment is quite safe, there are points on the human body where even a slight needle puncture could cause serious harm—in some cases, even death. Please bear in mind, my friends, that the puncture points we are talking about are only one-tenth of an inch in diameter and must be located, precisely located, before puncture is made."

At Voisin's direction, Dr. Altman took a needle from the alcohol-filled tray, waved it briefly in the air, and bent over Wolberg.

Voisin nodded, and Dr. Altman moved his head closer to Wolberg, held Wolberg's ear with his left thumb and forefinger. Wolberg winced—a nervous reaction, since the needle had not yet been inserted. Quickly, moving his wrist like someone throwing a dart, Altman pushed the needle into the tip of Wolberg's ear. Sampson flinched, but Wolberg apparently felt nothing.

"As I've indicated, each needle is inserted ten millimeters and remains *in situ* from five to ten minutes. Next." Altman again inserted a needle, into the ear lobe. Voisin looked, nodded. The procedure was repeated four more times, so that six needles protruded from in and around the ear.

Suddenly perspiring, Sampson mopped his forehead with a handkerchief. "And now, Dr. Abel, if you please." More talk by Voisin, most of which Sampson missed while staring at Wolberg. Abel bent over the patient, turned Wolberg's head slightly, and inserted a needle into his left jaw. "Stomach meridian, puncture three," continued Voisin. Sampson visibly shivered as Abel next bent Wolberg's nose just enough to insert a needle into the flesh next to his left nostril. Again Voisin nodded. Now Abel extended Wolberg's cheek between two fingers and slid a needle to rest under the left eye. A nerve twitched in Sampson's left cheek; unconsciously, he rubbed it. But Wolberg seemed insensate, gave no indication of feeling anything.

When Abel had finished, Voisin took his place beside Wolberg and slowly turned the patient's head so everyone might see. Looking unconcerned, even bored, Wolberg wore an even dozen needles in his ear, neck, cheek, inner ear, ear lobe, jaw, nose, and—almost—his eye. "As you can plainly see, my friends, no evidence of physical pain whatsoever." Voisin looked around defiantly, as though searching for contradiction. Finding an audience of believers, he returned to Wolberg. "Now the pulses. The duration of needle therapy is most frequently determined by the pulses. When the pulses register an improvement along the proper meridian, the needles are removed and the treatment has been successful."

Voisin motioned Wolberg into a reclining position, took his left wrist, and again concentrated as if listening. He nodded curtly, satisfied, and held Wolberg's wrist for Abel and Altman to feel. They took it in turn, said nothing, but also nodded. Then Voisin took the right wrist; again the victorious look. Quickly, he held up his hand to stop Altman from doing the same. "No time," he said as he began removing the needles.

Minus his needles, Wolberg sat up. Voisin examined his face briefly. There was not a single drop of blood. "How do you feel, Mr. Wolberg? Any pain?"

"No. None."

"Rest for a few moments. And drink this." The nurse handed a paper cup to Voisin, who sipped a bit before giving it to Wolberg. "No, gentlemen, no drugs. Just a simple protein solution which I have found mildly beneficial for most patients. A placebo, shall we say, that actually does some good."

Then it happened. Perhaps shyly conscious of eleven pairs of eyes fixed on his face, Wolberg blinked. It took Sampson endless seconds to record the significance of that fact. Both eyes had blinked. Sampson rubbed his own and stared at

21

Wolberg. A minute passed and, beyond doubt, Wolberg blinked again. Both eyes. "You see, *voilà!*" from the enraptured Voisin. Unaware of what all the fuss was about and bothered by Altman and Abel, who moved even closer to his face for a better view, Wolberg blinked for a third time. Abel and Altman looked at the audience and nodded. Then at Voisin and smiled. Embarrassed, like the man who doesn't understand a joke, Wolberg smiled, and when he smiled, the right side of his face edged upward. The audience of physicians were on their feet and, as a man, rushed to Wolberg. The woman—Voisin's "lovely skeptic"?—was not far behind.

Voisin was waving them back, mouthing volubly, and probably in French, thought Sampson, who could not distinguish many of the acupuncturist's words. Then he caught, "It is not much, one cannot hope for the miracles, but it is a beginning, yes? And with repeated treatment . . ." Someone's head blocked Voisin, and Sampson decided to join the celebration around the table. He had seen, and he believed.

It was in this party atmosphere that Abel waved to Sampson and advanced toward him, Dr. Altman in tow. "Sampson Trehune, I'd like to introduce Dr. Richard Altman, founder of the Altman Clinic and Connecticut's leading advocate of acupuncture." Altman snatched Sampson's hand and pumped it vigorously. "Mr. Trehune, of course. Yes. So glad you arrived in time to participate." Sampson grunted and withdrew his hand. "Come along and meet the rest of the boys," said Altman, turning and leading him into the heart of the crowd around the table. The men there were obviously physicians.

Performing the introductions, Altman forgot that Sampson was deaf, even though treatment for the condition was scheduled for later that day. "Mr. Trehune," Altman would say, smiling and looking directly at Sampson, "I'd like you to meet . . ." and Altman would turn his head as he spoke to

22

the person named. Said person, nameless as far as Sampson was concerned, would extend his hand, give Sampson's waiting hand a brief tug, and say "My pleasure, Mr. Trehune." Sampson grunted and nodded. What else could he do? Abel smiled, aware of Sampson's discomfort. Smoldering, Sampson retreated beyond the circle of hot light, back to his chair.

The dark was cool and calming. Casually surveying the room, he saw the woman. Was she another patient? Doubtful, or Abel would have mentioned her. She was standing next to the acupuncture chart, her make-up, hairdo, and clothes aggressively denying that she was over thirty-five. Her well-tailored, revealing dress of lavender print clashed with the gaudy reds and blues of the chart man's internal meridians.

Sampson studied her. When she spoke, as now to a doctor nearby, her lips moved rapidly and decisively, with full attention to each word. Otherwise, when her companion spoke, she seemed not to listen. *Seemed*. Her eyes, though apparently listless as they roamed the room, actually betrayed her close attention. At points in her partner's remarks, her eyes would stop, narrow to slits. When she spoke again, she was probably two steps ahead of her listener.

She may have felt Sampson's stare, for she turned sharply, focused on him, and waved. Silly woman. She left the pinstriped doctor and slid into the chair next to Sampson's. He turned to watch her speak but could only distinguish an occasional word because of the dim light. Periodically, he grunted, nodded. Apparently, that was enough. He was rescued from this one-sided blitz by Altman and Abel.

Speaking from the light and looking at him, Altman said, "Mr. Trehune, this is Claire Fletcher, one of the most influential journalists in the women's-magazine field." Sampson rose, jerked his head in her direction, and walked into the

23

light, forcing her to follow if she wanted to continue talking. Turning, he saw her say, ". . . believe in this acupuncture stuff." He shrugged his shoulders.

She turned to Altman. "What's he got? Is he the deaf one?" Abel to the rescue: "Mr. Trehune has been profoundly deaf since his ninth year, Miss Fletcher." Altman back to receive the pass: "But Dr. Voisin believes that he can be helped to hear again by applying the techniques of acupuncture."

"You sound like a press release," she said, with a snort. "My readers get enough puff pieces from other writers." The trio of men nodded and wished to be elsewhere. "Now if this works, fine. But seeing is believing and a blink or two is nothing. My readers have every right to the truth."

Altman again: "We invite skepticism, and have faith in your impartiality, Miss Fletcher, which is why you were allowed to be present today."

"Yeah!" Another snort. "That's not what you said last Monday. If it weren't for Dr. Eggers over there, you know I wouldn't be here."

"I assure you, Miss Fletcher, that given the current laws governing the practice of medicine in this state, the acupuncture treatment you have just witnessed might be considered, shall we say, unorthodox, and might be interpreted by some to be—"

She interrupted. "It's illegal. Say it. It doesn't take a rerun of *Frankenstein* to show the housewife that so-called disinterested science needs curbing."

Offensive rushing by Abel: "Two points, Miss Fletcher. Until the American Medical Association, through its lobby in Washington, permits the Supreme Court to rule on whether acupuncture is technically the practice of medicine, the question of legality is moot. The few cases which have reached the courts have been decided on grounds other than medical evidence."

Again she seemed not to be listening, but Sampson guessed she was taking mental notes as rapidly as Abel spoke, and he would wager she could repeat Abel's comments with unerring accuracy. A prodigious memory, no doubt.

But Abel plowed on. "And as far as the experimental stage of acupuncture is concerned, Miss Fletcher, the charts you see have been used to cure people for over four thousand years. Would that our drug companies waited for such lengthy field testing before releasing their sometimes dubious products. When one considers that one-fourth of the world's population positively thrives on this treatment—well, the word 'experimental' becomes questionable."

"Excuse me, gotta talk to Wolberg." She left abruptly.

Abel and Sampson followed her, arriving in time to see Voisin say, "Not now, please. Mr. Wolberg should rest for a while. You may ask him anything you want, but later, yes?"

"Sure," she drawled and strode away. That would be quite a contest.

Sampson nodded at Wolberg, enunciating, "Hi, Harry, you looked swell." Wolberg smiled. Voisin turned sharply to Sampson and stared at him, without speaking, for an uncomfortably long time. Finally, "You are Mr. Trehune; as soon as I have Mr. Wolberg resting, we will talk." Voisin left with Wolberg, entering one of the small treatment rooms off the operating arena. He returned quickly.

"Dr. Abel, please, it is necessary that I speak with Mr. Trehune privately. You understand the importance of questioning. To save time, if you, Dr. Altman, and the others could have a cup of coffee, perhaps? Something. This will not be extensive in Mr. Trehune's case. No more than half an hour." Not waiting for Abel's reply, he took Sampson by the arm and led him to a second treatment room where, indicating Sampson was to take the chair, he perched atop the table.

"And now, Mr. Trehune, I am Henri Voisin. You must tell me about yourself; everything, you understand?" Sampson began carefully reciting in his best voice the list of childhood diseases he had fallen victim to. "Influenza at eight. That was 1937, bad epidemic. Hospitalized, complications, scarlet fever set in. Woke up one day, could not hear." Voisin nodded, staring intently at Sampson as he talked. "You have had other treatment?" he asked. Sampson began again, wearily. "Marvelous fenestration procedure at Johns Hopkins, did not work. Tympanoplasty of middle-ear tissue, also did not work. And Dr. Nathan Ross, quite prominent, performed a delicate operation in microscopic surgery in attempt to activate the foot plate of the stapes by a direct incision through the outer ear after cutting past the eardrum."

Sampson had to pause to regroup. Concentration took a lot out of him, and this was the longest speech he had made in some time. Voisin nodded understandingly and waited. "That operation much talked about, but I could not hear talk. I am permanently deaf."

"You also feel sorry for yourself, Mr. Trehune. But that is a minor point." Still the stare, as though he were looking right into Sampson's organs. He got off the table and felt Sampson's arms, legs, chest, and back. He poked into his ears, pulled back his eyelids and gazed deeply. Sampson saw him wrinkle his nose a couple of times, as though he were smelling.

"Anything else?"

"Broke an arm once. Lost two teeth in a fall. Getting too fat." The last with a self-deprecating grin.

Voisin became impatient, as though he already knew all this and didn't want to waste time. "And you do not get enough rest, you are far too nervous, you not only eat too much but the food is far too rich. Perhaps most important, you drink too much."

Sampson felt cheated and angry, just as he had when Voisin announced Wolberg's nervousness. "Good guess," he agreed.

Voisin turned from gray to pink, obviously enraged. He glared down at Sampson. "Acupuncture is not a guess! I never guess. Never!" Voisin paced; Sampson lowered his eyes. Finally, Voisin: "Dr. Abel tells me that you are a dealer in rare books, that you have read much about acupuncture. Is that true?" Sampson nodded contritely.

"Raise your right trouser leg and point to the liver meridian. Can you do that?" Sampson obeyed, pointing to a spot about midway down his right calf. "Is that sore?" Sampson shook his head no.

"Good. Now take your first finger and push it into your leg—top, side, bottom, anyplace but the liver meridian."

Puzzled, Sampson prodded his leg.

"Feel anything?"

"Nope."

"Now push your finger directly into the liver meridian," Voisin ordered and smiled. Sampson did and gasped, giving voice to some animal cry of pain. "So, so," said Voisin, if anything, smiling more broadly. "Did I not tell you so? Listen to me. You think because I have no stethoscope or X-ray film I am a fool, that I know nothing. Bah! In eight years' time, exactly eight years, if you do not change your drinking habits, you will have a severe liver disease! You felt the malfunction of the meridian yourself. You think you can hide such things? I don't even need to take the pulses. I can see your liver in the color of your eyes, I can feel it in your ribs, I can hear it when you breathe. I can even smell your decaying liver. Remember, eight years, that's all the time you have left. And if you don't stop drinking, you're a fool."

Voisin paused for breath and then added to the astounded

Sampson, "But we shall probably be able to make you a fool that hears, at least." Pause. Voisin glanced at his watch. "And now, Mr. Trehune, if you will excuse me, I must check on Mr. Wolberg."

Sampson, alone with his thoughts, could almost feel his liver decaying as the minutes ticked away. He wished he had a drink. He got up and walked to the doorway. Abel and the doctors were standing beside the acupuncture chart. Voisin was nowhere to be seen. Sampson wandered to the next treatment room for a word with Wolberg. He stopped short in the doorway.

Wolberg was spread-eagled on the floor. Voisin was kneeling beside him, nervously feeling his pulses. In his right hand, he held an acupuncture needle. Voisin began shaking his head, and continued shaking it madly. Sampson turned and waved to Abel, frantic. Abel, followed by two of the doctors, scurried across the operating arena toward the treatment room.

Voisin was still kneeling beside Wolberg when they arrived, and Abel, placing an arm around him, helped him to his feet. Voisin still shook his head. One of the doctors dropped to his knees and seized Wolberg's wrist, searching for a pulse. "Coronary. Get Altman, quick." The other doctor was about to leave when Altman appeared in the doorway, accompanied by Miss Fletcher. "Coronary. Need electric stimulator, quick," the kneeling doctor reiterated. "This way," said Altman, and helped carry the sagging body of Wolberg into a third room.

Doctors milled around the doorway so Sampson could not see what was happening. At last, Altman and Abel emerged from the crowd, heads down. "It was too late. Nothing could be done," said Altman.

"You did your best, but time was against you."

"Bob," Altman said, "you know what this means? I'll have

to notify the police. Even if we wanted to, with Fletcher here there's no way to keep this quiet."

The other doctors, catching the drift of his statements, exchanged literally horrified glances. Police investigating a death under suspicious circumstances in a room full of physicians was anathema. They scurried for telephones and the reassurance of their lawyers.

Abel remained behind to speak with Sampson. "Coronary. Not related to the acupuncture treatment or, if so, only indirectly," he signed. Sampson nodded. "But I was his physician and it didn't seem to me that his heart was so weak." Abel was plainly worried.

Just then Sampson noticed Voisin enter the room where Wolberg's body had been left. He and Abel followed. Voisin was clutching Wolberg's right wrist with the same intense look upon his face, feeling, listening. Seeing them, he shook his head, but remained silent a moment longer, still gripping Wolberg's wrist. Then he faced them squarely and said simply, "No. The pulses don't lie. No."

Sampson questioned, "But can you read pulses after death?"

"The deep pulses do not cease for some time after death. And Wolberg's deep pulses do not indicate a coronary. That is what I was trying to determine when you came charging in. There is still a reading of massive disturbance along the stomach meridian. Harrison Wolberg did not die of a coronary attack."

Voisin looked positive. Abel looked shocked. Sampson felt that he himself probably looked confused. He went to find a place to sit and gather his thoughts. Better call T.J., he reflected. This may be a long night.

29

THREE

Panic! Fighting up from the depths of sleep, Sampson Trehune found himself in a strange bed. God, how he hated the instant of awakening in alien surroundings. He reconstructed: a bed in the Blue Coat Hotel, in Hastings, Connecticut, in the United States. He sighed heavily. His eyes felt gummy; his head ached and his mouth tasted foul. Not from too much Scotch, worse luck; there had been only one ever-so-polite nightcap in Dr. Altman's private office after Harrison Wolberg's body had been removed temporarily to another part of the clinic, after the police had finished their nagging questions. During that time—almost six hours—he had smoked, finishing two packs of a wretched brand he purchased from a machine in the clinic's cafeteria.

And he had talked and talked. The zealous and suspicious Lieutenant Alvin Hodges, chief of Hastings's police force—eleven men full-time, six part-time—had been adamant about procedure. Sampson had struggled over a preliminary statement without assistance from Abel. "We like to take our statements one by one, Mr.—aaahh—Mr. Trehune. That way there's no confusion later about who said what. I'm sure you understand." Sampson understood only that it took him an hour to answer the lieutenant's questions and to part-dictate, part-write a statement.

His sluggish gaze took in the face of Robert Abel, a face attached to an arm which was shaking him gently but determinedly into awareness of an obscenely bright October morning. The drapes which covered the windows had been pulled back, and Abel was deluged in sunlight. He seemed to wear a nimbus.

"Good morning," the doctor said. "You've got half an hour. Better hurry." Sampson nodded grumpily, but didn't move. With a sanctimonious air, Abel reported that he had been up for some time and that he had taken a brisk walk to the local drugstore over a mile away to purchase a razor, toothbrushes, and toothpaste. He nodded toward the bathroom where he had left them for Sampson.

As Sampson watched, Abel's cheeks puffed and his lips rounded until he resembled a goldfish Sampson once had who had died of overfeeding. He's whistling, Sampson thought with disgust, being barely able to recall the sensation from his childhood but aware that Hearers performed such an act when they were happy or nervous or both. Whistling! He's enjoying this. Abel switched on the television set to watch a morning talk program where purple, green, and orange-pink people moved their lips excitedly. Sampson lit a cigarette, closed his eyes, and was alone.

Not expecting to spend the night in Hastings, he had not brought along his personal alarm clock, a wind-up timer which could be set anywhere up to twelve hours and placed beneath his pillow. At the appointed hour, the timer would go off, striking every five seconds, sending out waves of vibrations which usually awakened him.

There had been a scene last night at the desk when he checked in. Since pounding on his door or persistent phone calls could not awaken him, Sampson demanded both keys to his room, intending to give one to Abel. Behind the desk, a smug young man objected. A badge he wore identified him as Timothy Anderson, desk clerk—night. "Sorry, sir, but hotel policy prohibits giving both room keys to guests."

Abel tried to explain; Sampson explained further with a

five-dollar bill. He now had a friend for as long as he stayed in Hastings. "You shouldn't always try to buy people," Abel had remonstrated. "Reason with them. This reinforces their individual sense of—" Sampson slammed the door.

A cigarette ash burned his finger, and he opened his eyes seaching for an ashtray. On the bedside table he spied a brass colonial something-or-other and ground out the butt. An *objet d'art*, no doubt, bought wholesale from a Far East importer.

"Better hurry." Abel was at the foot of the bed, oozing sincerity and bonhomie. Once a doctor, always a doctor.

"Why?" Sampson signed lazily.

"The Assistant County Prosecutor is going to meet us at the desk and drive us over to the courthouse."

Sampson nodded and made a move to get out of bed, and Abel left. As soon as his friend was gone, however, Sampson slumped back on his pillows and lit another cigarette.

When the police had departed the night before, the physicians had gathered in Altman's office for their own postmortem: hands were wrung, angry words exchanged, a recrimination or two thrown about. The names of the A.M.A. and various county medical societies were taken in vain. A prayer of thanks was offered to the Deity for his foresight in making Hastings such a small, out-of-the-way place, with little chance of publicity. If only that Fletcher woman would keep her mouth shut. Each doctor had logged his personal complaints.

"Do you realize," Abel had said, "what it's going to mean to a patient when I am forced to miss his appointment tomorrow?"

"A free hour when he can sit down, have a quiet drink, and relax," Sampson had suggested, then retreated. He hated crowds. With one person, Sampson had no problem understanding what was said; with two, some slight difficulty.

32

When three Hearers talked, usually at the same time, he felt like a referee whose calls were being ignored. With a room full of people—and despite the generous size of Altman's office suite, seven worried physicians did make a room full—it was chaos, like trying to watch a dozen Ping-Pong matches simultaneously. He had sought out the cigarette machine in the cafeteria and sat for a few minutes, smoking and thinking.

This morning he thought about the same subject: Henri Voisin. Rather than follow the lead of the other doctors, Voisin had vigorously contradicted them. In a busybody fashion, he had got in the way of the police at nearly every turn, insisting that, according to the acupuncture pulses, Wolberg had not died from a coronary. Lieutenant Hodges, Sampson thought, had shown remarkable restraint.

And then the bit about the extra needle. When the police had concluded their examination of the operating area and adjoining treatment rooms, Voisin had waxed frantic again. "There is an extra needle here! Lieutenant Hodges, there is an extra needle."

A petite blond nurse, one Nancy Something-or-Other, was questioned briefly. She had performed as a general factotum for Altman, tucking in sheets, passing out extra copies of each patient's abbreviated medical history. She had remained for the treatment of Wolberg. At Voisin's direction, she filled a shallow tray with alcohol, in which he sterilized the acupuncture needles. The tray was placed on a small metal stand near the treatment table. No, she had not counted the needles. Why should she?

"But, sir," reiterated Voisin in desperate politeness, "I had sterilized eighteen needles at the beginning of my treatment. Now, when I dry them and put them away, I find I have nineteen."

The lieutenant was unimpressed. "Well, perhaps you made a mistake," he suggested unwisely.

33

Voisin exploded. "I do not make mistakes! You think I am one of your so-called doctors who can't count the number of sponges or scalpels in an operation and sews them up inside a patient? I am an *acuponcteur!*" He used the French term and seemed to grow taller and straighter as he spoke. Shades of the Grand Charles. "You, sir, are a bungler," Voisin had concluded and sat down. He had said next to nothing for the rest of the night.

Sampson glanced at his watch now, put thoughts of needles from his mind. He would have to hurry. He trundled into the bathroom and turned on the shower. Spare tire, he rebuked himself—as usual. When he got out of the shower, he scrubbed the steam from the mirror. He actually looked at his reflection for the first time in days. A heavily bearded face, but smooth. Complexion more sallow than usual. A smallish mouth with mobile lips. A quirky nose. Thick, wavy black hair, without a part. Not bad, he thought, straightening a tangled eyebrow. He shaved. Five minutes later, having cursed his limp shirt, he was out the door of his room.

Not bad, he thought again. He was looking at a pair of trim legs bent over a suitcase in the doorway of the next room. The legs disappeared into the room, the door ajar. Sampson stood in the doorway and looked.

She was alone in the room. About five feet seven, he estimated, plus two inches for heels. She would reach his forehead. Rich, glossy chestnut hair fell to her shoulders. She wore an understated black suit. Briskly she pulled out drawers, then poked her head into the bathroom and closet. She opened a briefcase on the made-up bed and tossed in two bulging manila envelopes. She turned and met Sampson's eyes.

"Yes? Is there something I can do for you?"

Sampson was charmed. Obviously she had taken elocution lessons—probably at a "good" Eastern prep school—and had done a good bit of public speaking. She used her mouth well.

Her "th" especially was a delight, her tongue darting out from between her white teeth and crimson lips as if she were delicately devouring an ice-cream cone. She was just over thirty, with a girlish—almost tomboy—look. Mary Pickford had been described as no longer a girl, not yet a woman, Sampson recalled. But this was a woman. The curves were just to his taste.

"Well, are you deaf!" It wasn't a question. She gathered up a gray knit coat. Her shoulders pulled back slightly; anger flared in her eyes.

Ignoring her words, Sampson read her presence. She could be formidable.

"I said—are you deaf!" Her mouth showed that she hung on to each word. She was about to lose her temper.

"Yes. I am."

Her blush never had a chance. "You read lips well," she said, picking up her briefcase.

"Practice," he said, bending down for the suitcase in the doorway. God, it was heavy. "You speak well."

"Practice. I've never met a deaf person before," she added. Her green eyes reached dispassionately into his.

"Only three million of us in the country," Sampson offered. "Hardly enough to go around."

She closed the door, first checking her purse for the key. They walked in silence down the wide, circular stairway. Sampson paused to change his grip on the suitcase.

"You travel well equipped."

"That's not mine." She didn't explain, but looked at him curiously. "I bet deaf people are very intelligent observers. They must notice things others miss."

"Sharp, very sharp," Sampson agreed. Without pause, he launched into a well-rehearsed account of that day in 1911 when Alexander Graham Bell of telephone fame mounted a platform in New York to deliver the first of many lectures on his most controversial idea: the deliberate breeding of a separate human species—the totally deaf. Because of their heightened remaining senses, Bell reasoned, the deaf would soon exhibit superhuman capabilities.

"He was right, too," Sampson concluded. "Many feats performed by Sherlock Holmes commonplace, child's play, for deaf person. Be surprised."

"I bet I would."

Thus flattered, he was about to continue.

"Got to run," she cut him off. "Would you please leave the bag at the desk? They'll hold it for me. Thanks so much." Shamelessly, Sampson watched until her hips disappeared through the double glass doors.

He picked up the bag, straightened his shoulders, and marched to the desk. He always felt expansive, almost inspired, when he thought of Bell. An attractive, attentive audience made it all the better.

"Working long hours?" queried Sampson.

"Have to, with all this police fuss." Anderson, the desk clerk, winked. "See you met our Miss Shaw."

"Manager?"

"God, no, and thank God twice," said Anderson. "Belinda Shaw's our Assistant County Prosecutor. She's in charge of the Wolberg case." The clerk lifted the bag from the desk, and Sampson noticed the gold initials "H.W." Harrison Wolberg. Elementary, my dear Watson.

As he walked across the lobby and down a hall leading to Ye Olde Colonial Restaurante, he felt like a suddenly pricked balloon. He had planned literally and figuratively to play dumb at the Medical Examiner's hearing today. Get out of answering a lot of fool questions. Quite simple. Sampson was a master at conning people, at appearing a trifle feebleminded. It wasn't a talent he boasted about, since Hearers were notoriously simple at times. Still, it was useful, especially when you didn't want to answer questions from a County Prosecutor.

He was waved into a vacant chair by Abel, who was engrossed in a discussion with two other physicians. Abel introduced him, both pronouncing and spelling their names. "Dr. Karl Muntz," he said and followed it quickly with "M-u-n-t-z." And "Dr. Hector Delgado." He used the finger alphabet again. They both nodded, then continued their discussion while Sampson glanced at the menu. He pointed a finger to "Ye Olde Colonial Speciale," otherwise known as bacon and eggs.

When the waitress left, Sampson snagged Abel's attention. "Why didn't you tell me she was a woman?" he signed furiously.

Abel's glance followed the waitress and returned to Sampson, puzzled. "The waitress?" his fingers asked.

Sampson kicked him under the table. "No, not the waitress, dolt! The County Prosecutor."

Looking amused, Abel signed, "I didn't think you would care. She sounded quite charming, hardly a cause for panic." Sampson scowled and they both returned to the general discussion which, naturally, was about acupuncture.

Hector Delgado was especially concerned, since he had long championed the needles as inexpensive and quick medical care for New York's ever-increasing Puerto Rican population. "Have you known Dr. Voisin long?" he asked everyone in general.

Sampson shook his head. Abel explained how he had met the acupuncturist once before, about three months ago, when Voisin had first arrived in the States.

Dr. Muntz, who was an elderly man, stared into the tablecloth, making small circles with his index finger. When he spoke, Abel had to translate surreptitiously for Sampson.

Despite nearly two decades in New York, Muntz had preserved his German accent intact and his words only confused Sampson. "No, no," Abel signed his words, "I have never met him. And yet—"

"Yet" was forgotten when Belinda Shaw crossed the room and spoke to the men at the table, introducing herself. Sampson rose with the others, and nodded sheepishly as she called him by name. Obediently, they followed her from the restaurant. The waitress had just brought Sampson's coffee as he started to leave. He gulped a mouthful, burned his tongue, scalded his throat, and cursed aloud. The poor woman in her red-and-blue pseudo-colonial uniform was genuinely shocked. He left a large tip.

Although the Blue Coat was on the outskirts of Hastings, clusters of people had gathered at both corners, and several cars were parked across the street. A young man with severe acne and a green corduroy coat held up a camera as they passed him. Four red-and-white Fords, dome lights spinning, lined the hotel driveway.

Shaw led the way to the first squad car. Abel, Delgado, and Sampson were ushered into the rear seat. Lieutenant Hodges, bright-eyed despite the ordeal of the night before, held the door for them. When he closed it, Sampson noted that there were no handles on the inside. He started to feel claustrophobic. Straining to look through the rear window, he saw Dr. Eggers, with Claire Fletcher in tow—or, more probably, vice versa—follow Dr. Muntz into the next squad car.

Hodges slid into the driver's seat; Belinda Shaw sat beside him. As the car pulled away, she turned her head and began talking. The wire mesh which separated the rear and front seats obscured most of her words, fueling Sampson's claustrophobia. As they drove down Hastings's main street—cleverly named Main Street, Sampson noted—he caught only a few of

38

her words. Apparently she pointed out places where George Washington had slept, or at least stopped to water his horse.

Aside from being the county seat, Hastings had little to recommend it, from what Sampson could see. Reading his expression, Shaw added that the pace of Hastings should pick up once Bannon Electronics resumed full employment. But the courthouse, at the opposite end of town from the hotel, was a pleasant surprise. No rusty cannon on the lawn, or statues of Minutemen and past mayors. No stately imitation-marble columns. Just a rambling three-story frame structure which had once served as a mansion and now housed both the city and the county judiciary. A simple sign at the edge of the well-trimmed lawn announced, "COURTHOUSE."

Tagging along behind Shaw down the short second-floor corridor, Sampson watched her with interest. She strode easily, assuredly, greeting people left and right and receiving smiles and friendly nods in return. She was in her element here, he thought. Or at least one of her elements, he added, noting again the gentle sway of her hips as she turned in to an open double door marked by a plain wooden plaque: "ROOM 4."

Shaw led them to a row of chairs and sallied to the front of the room, which was divided roughly in half by a limp red velvet rope. There were only rows of chairs on the side where Sampson sat. On the other, there was a plain desk on a raised platform. Directly to the right of the platform was a comfortable wing chair. Two tables, each with four chairs, stood forward on either side of the desk. To Sampson's left, French doors led into the bright October sunlight. The setting, which filled rapidly, was reminiscent of a drawing room rather than a courtroom.

A gaunt, emaciated man, who might have posed for an American Gothic poster, stationed himself in front of the platform. Everyone rose as he introduced the Honorable . . .

"Haemen Holmes," Abel spelled. The judge was casually dressed in a sports jacket of salt-and-pepper tweed. He lowered his stocky frame into the chair behind the desk. Next, Altman and two unknowns filed in and sat at the table to the left of the judge. They were followed by Belinda Shaw and Lieutenant Hodges, who sat on the right. The judge ran a hand through his longish, graying hair. He nodded, and the hearing began.

For Sampson, the next hour was utter confusion, in spite of the courtroom's orderliness. Too many Hearers bent on doing their thing. The judge scribbled notes with his right hand while resting his chin in his left. His lips were obscured. The craned heads in front of Sampson blocked Shaw, which really made little difference. Her back was usually turned while she questioned the witnesses.

Sampson did understand that Altman was the County Medical Examiner. Two local physicians who had not been present at the acupuncture demonstration backed his sworn statement with their testimony. Wolberg's death had resulted from heart failure, which was totally unrelated to the acupuncture treatment—so far as they could tell, the two locals hedged. But they knew their stuff. Certainly they would have caught anything even slightly suspicious.

Abel's fingers recited a portion of Altman's statement which received special attention. He had administered an electrocardiogram to Wolberg a week before the acupuncture session. Wolberg's heart was "performing as well as could be expected." Wolberg, who had suffered a stroke, was indeed a victim of hypertension and high blood pressure. But not dangerously so. Besides, acupuncture was not the least traumatic.

The doctors who had been present for Wolberg's acupuncture treatment testified next, and Sampson temporarily lost his interpreter. Abel confirmed Wolberg's brief fling at psychoanalysis some six months before. Sampson could barely read his answers to Shaw's questions, which, of course, he could not see.

Yes, before analysis began, Wolberg had a complete physical. Given his age and general condition, nothing out-of-the-ordinary was discovered. Certainly nothing to indicate an incipient coronary.

Yes, Wolberg had problems, but nothing unusual for his age and position.

No, he discontinued analysis after only eight sessions. He offered no explanation for quitting except that he was very busy.

"Improvement? Impossible to say."

Finally, Shaw handed Abel a paper. After reading it, he said, "Yes, that is the statement I made regarding the events of last night, and it is correct. No, I do not wish to change or add anything."

Abel was replaced by Dr. Charles Eggers, who kept smiling at Claire Fletcher while he answered Shaw's questions, almost like a child seeking approval. Since neither he nor any of the physicians except Abel and Altman had known or treated Wolberg, their evidence was a rehash of earlier testimony about last night's proceedings. Only their mannerisms separated them.

Delgado's gestures were characteristically Latin. Dr. John Mosley nervously stabbed at his brow with a king-size handkerchief. "He holds a chair at the University of Connecticut," Abel signed. Evidently, he feared that the Board of Trustees would not understand his participation in a faintly illegal procedure like acupuncture.

The chair next to the judge was vacant. American Gothic spoke to the audience, but Sampson missed what he said. "Hurley—Dr. James Hurley," Abel explained. "He doesn't seem to be present." A man exuding the assurance of Caesar addressing his legions rose and spoke to the bench. Abel summarized for Sampson. "Ho. Hurley's been called away. A desperate case, probably one of his wealthy Bridgeport widows. That's his lawyer. Hurley will be available later, if absolutely necessary." The lawyer sat down, Shaw burned, the judge scratched his chin.

Bridgeport was in another county, and technically Hurley had deliberately fled Shaw's jurisdiction. Yet Hurley, obviously, had powerful friends. Sampson was willing to wager a Gutenberg Bible that Shaw would proceed cautiously no matter how angry she was.

She nodded toward the lawyer, spoke briefly to Judge Holmes, and, with a shrug of her shapely shoulders, proceeded with the hearing.

Claire Fletcher, the next witness, was wearing yesterday's dress. Must bother her, thought Sampson. Out of place. She took a loose-leaf notebook from her purse, flipped it open, and succinctly answered Shaw's questions. She sat and spoke like the Ultimate Computer. Sampson could see the antagonism building between the journalist and Shaw. Canny bitch, he thought partisanly. But before surrendering the witness chair, Fletcher was unable to resist making a speech.

"As I explained previously, my presence at the Altman Clinic last night was for the purpose of investigating the subject of acupuncture and informing my readers of any danger inherent in such treatment. If the events of last night are any indication, my warnings to the American public will be timely indeed."

The judge cut her off and the Ultimate Computer short-circuited. Only her awareness of probable audience response prevented her from exploding. Bet she knows her statement will hit the wire services and make news, Sampson thought.

He closed his eyes, feeling the dull throb of an oncoming headache. Not just from so much concentration on the Hearers' world. He had missed his usual four cups of morning coffee. "You're addicted to caffeine," Abel had once pronounced. He was probably right.

42

When Sampson opened his eyes, Henri Voisin was on the stand. The acupuncturist was halfway through a gesture of disdain, if not outright contempt. He finished the imperious wave of his hand that was directed toward the American Gothic clerk, who approached him with a small leather Bible. The astonished man stopped in midstep and looked toward the judge, who lifted his head and motioned the clerk away. For the first time, the judge looked alert.

"You are Henri Voisin?" the judge asked.

"Dr. Henri Voisin, yes. I will speak the truth, I assure you, even if you do not wish to hear it."

Here we go; never mind the headache. Just as he turned to Abel, Sampson saw jaws flapping, others simply hanging open.

"What?" he poked Abel in the ribs, signing anxiously. "What? What?"

"The judge asked Voisin if he's a Communist."

"And?"

"He said that he was a doctor, that any doctor who was not a Communist was either a hypocrite or a fool."

Sampson pressed his eyelids shut. A Quixote. A damn Don Quixote, with an acupuncture needle for a lance. This was the man who was going to make him hear again. Voisin's words echoed through his mind, "A fool who can hear, at least." He was a fool all right.

He looked up, expecting the worst, but instead found the judge, Shaw, Lieutenant Hodges, even Dr. Hurley's lawyer—all gazing raptly at Voisin, who was standing. An acupuncture needle shimmered in his fingers. He explained briefly the principles underlying the ancient Chinese practice. Then, without any warning, he smoothly plunged the needle into his cheek and left it dangling.

But he continued to speak. He described the flow of *Ch'i*, the universal energy, through the body's meridians; then he

43

produced a second needle and slipped it into his other cheek. He turned full face to the judge, then back to Shaw.

"My apologies for such a cheap, theatrical trick. I assure you needle therapy is no parlor trick, no illusion. It is as demonstrably effective as any branch of Western medicine. And for my learned colleagues to imply that inserting needles along the meridians of the gall bladder and the stomach produced a change in the unfortunate Mr. Wolberg's heart—why, they are even bigger fools than I had heretofore thought." Sampson felt the anger and resentment swirl around him. He saw people leaning forward, muttering to themselves or to each other. Needles embedded in each cheek, Voisin continued unperturbed.

"Indeed, it is curious that Wolberg died at all, since his pulses were perfectly normal when I read them less than a half-hour before his death. And it is more curious that my Western colleagues ignore even the primitive means at their disposal. I refer, of course, to an autopsy. This lovely woman" —Voisin indicated Shaw—"not only denied the possibility of his death from other causes, but she told us that she will release Wolberg's body. Why? Because the family is Jewish and their Orthodox Jewish faith prohibits an autopsy. Primitive procedure thwarted by even more primitive superstition!"

The judge looked for a gavel, discovered he had none. He pounded his fist on the desk. American Gothic waved his arms. Several people in the audience stood up. Hodges's face showed consternation. But still Voisin continued. As he stepped forward, the needles quivered in his cheeks.

"Is there something to hide? What of the nineteenth needle? Will no one answer me?"

The judge answered. Contempt of court. The clerk, along with two of Lieutenant Hodges's policemen who had hurried to the front of the courtroom, took hold of Voisin. The doctor regarded them with something near amusement. He

44

shook his arms free and calmly removed the needles from his cheeks.

Abel poked Sampson in the ribs, indicating they should leave. "The judge said to clear the room at once," he signed. On the way out, the pair was stopped by Shaw. Altman's nurse stood beside her. "Mr. Trehune, your testimony, along with Nurse Harmon's, will be taken in chambers. Please follow me." She led them out through the double doors, into the crowd milling about the hall.

Claire Fletcher pounced on them there. "Well, dearie," she said to Shaw, "it looks like you've got a problem. Pity you couldn't sweep it under the rug at your friendly little hearing." Shaw glared, and made a move to walk around her. The young man with acne and a camera temporarily blocked her, attempting to snap a photograph of her, Sampson, and Nurse Harmon. Shaw said something which Sampson didn't see. The photographer backed away, flapping. "Freedom of the press, Miss Shaw. You can't interfere with the people's right to know."

"That's right"—Fletcher jumped in again—"and those anti-Semitic slurs that were made in the courtroom are certainly newsworthy. Just what are you going to do about this? After all, Voisin may have a point or two, even if he hates Jews. Don't you think, Miss Prosecutor, that this whole hearing was just a little too, too cozy? What about that drink Wolberg took when they pulled the needles out? I was there and saw it, you know, the whole thing. What about that drink?"

Shaw stood erect, but gripped her briefcase more tightly. "One of our policemen took the crushed paper cup and Dr. Voisin's bottle to Hartford last night, where the state police lab analyzed it. The contents were precisely what Voisin claimed them to be—orange juice and a vitamin-protein supplement. That state lab report was on my desk this morning, before the Medical Examiner's hearing convened. Sorry to disappoint you. You'll have to look elsewhere for headlines."

Fletcher didn't give an inch. "I suppose you still won't demand an autopsy?"

"I believe Lieutenant Hodges is now taking the appropriate steps to have the remains of Harrison Wolberg examined by the proper medical authorities."

"Hastings's own Dr. Richard Altman being the 'proper authority,' no doubt. Really, you'll have to do better than that."

"We have," Shaw said, smiling. "Earlier this morning, Dr. Altman asked to be relieved from his post as County Medical Examiner should an autopsy be necessary. The state pathologist, Dr. L. L. Parsons, is already on his way. He'll arrive this afternoon from Bridgeport and begin the autopsy immediately. You can read all about it in the newspapers."

With Sampson, Harmon, and Abel in file behind her, Shaw led the way to Judge Holmes's chambers, where they found him pacing the floor, jacket off, and perspiring slightly. Judge Holmes knew political dynamite when he was sitting on it. "I don't like this, Belinda. I don't like this a bit. But I suppose we'd better get on with it."

Nurse Nancy Harmon, dressed in uniform and cap, a navy-blue sweater tossed over her shoulders and held in place by a pearl chain, was first. Dr. Altman and his two companions joined them. Harmon's testimony was as crisp and assured as her starched white dress; without hesitation, she described her part in the previous evening's affair, capably fielding questions put to her by Shaw and Altman.

Thanks to Shaw, Sampson was allowed to use Abel as an interpreter. He closed his eyes. The events of the night before filled his mind and ran through his fingers. Replaying a silent film, he ticked off the people, movements, and impressions he had stored. Surprising detail, but no new, solid information. He signed copies of the statement he had made to Lieutenant Hodges, then left.

46

"Bar don't open till twelve sharp," said the waitress at Ye Olde Colonial Restaurante. "But I'll see what I can do." Obviously, she'd heard of Sampson's generosity.

"We shouldn't have bothered," he signed to Abel, as they finished their lunch. The Scotch-on-the-rocks was composed almost entirely of rocks; the Spirite of '76 Burger would have given George Washington himself second thoughts.

At 3:05 they boarded the 2:15 for New York, and discovered that Drs. Delgado and Eggers, as well as Claire Fletcher, were also returning. They reversed a coach seat, Abel and Sampson on one side, Delgado, Fletcher, and Eggers on the other. Dr. Muntz passed them, nodded, and retired to the end of the car.

The seat across the aisle from Sampson held Harrison Wolberg's suitcase and a briefcase. Since Abel was acquainted with the Wolberg family, he had offered to take Harrison's personal effects back to the city. They had been thoroughly cataloged and Abel had been obliged to sign a lengthy receipt.

The conversation pushed forward, slowly and clumsily, keeping pace with the train, which eventually jerked to a stop at Darien. The four men left their seats and roamed in search of the bar car. They found it. Dilapidated, smelly, and scarred. They were served drinks resentfully, and then they retreated to the rear of the car so as not to disturb the meditations of the porter.

As the train proceeded on its way, Abel and Delgado discussed socialized medicine or some such heresy, and Sampson was left with Eggers. After ten minutes of smiles and pretentious nothings from the doctor, Sampson concluded that the man was a complete ass, and deserved anything Claire Fletcher could do to him. Eggers described a jolly good round of golf which he had played last summer—or perhaps it was the summer before—until Sampson deserted him and headed back to his seat.

47

As he walked past Dr. Muntz, the old man looked up at Sampson as if he wanted to say something. Remembering the thick accent, Sampson kept going. He was about to flop into his seat when he noticed that Claire Fletcher had two brown envelopes on her lap. She was busy trying to remove the sticky tape which sealed them. She looked up at him, grinned, then continued to pry the tape loose with her fingernails. The briefcase on the seat across the aisle was open.

What the hell should he do, Sampson wondered. Scream for a cop? Rush to get Abel? Snatch them from her thieving hands?

"Sit down, Mr. Trehune," she said pleasantly. "You make me nervous standing there." Obediently, he sat next to her. "You don't like me, do you?" Sampson didn't contradict her. "Figures. I'm in a dirty business, and I don't stay on top by being polite. If a Washington columnist can score a scoop by going through the garbage cans of J. Edgar Hoover—well, I figure there might be a story in the lint from Harrison Wolberg's pockets, if you know what I mean." He said nothing, still debating what he should do.

"Here, hold this," she ordered, and handed him the envelope. She had loosened the flap and tape just enough to shake its contents onto her lap. She studied the items and passed them to Sampson. "Put them back. Don't tear the envelope any more than it already is."

The dregs of a man's life, Sampson thought sadly, but he examined them anyway. A thin leather holder for a batch of credit cards; a matching wallet; four paper clips; receipts for a rented car; a small envelope with two tickets for a performance—last Wednesday's—of a recent Broadway hit, one distinguished by an entirely nude athletic cast. Three pocket-sized notebooks, shiny orange covers with splotches where something had been spilled over them. Two were unused; one had several pages torn from the front, little bits of paper

48

still caught in the wire spiral. A clean white linen handkerchief. A ring filled with keys. A gold pen-and-pencil set. A cheap ballpoint pen with its end chewed. A small yellow lead pencil with the point worn down.

Next Fletcher passed him a comb, a gold money clip in the shape of a ticker-tape machine, and a sealed white envelope marked "CASH," with "$84.14" written across the flap and initialed. He slipped the items back into the brown envelope, which the woman then resealed with spit and a bit of Scotch tape.

"Not a damn thing that I can see. Nothing."

Sampson nodded, and was about to ask her just what she had expected to find when Abel and Delgado and Eggers returned. Three merry mouseketeers of medicine, bumping down the aisle, Sampson thought disdainfully, amusing himself with the picture. They gathered their belongings. Sampson exchanged a glance with Fletcher, who was watching him, tense, alert: You were in it, too, her look said. Abel peered briefly at Wolberg's things but did not touch them.

As they stepped down from their one-time silver coach at Grand Central and walked along the steam-misted platform to the station itself, no one said a word. In the station, there was a moment, brief and false, of good fellowship before they went their separate ways.

Eggers and Fletcher hailed old Dr. Muntz, leading him off to God knew what. Delgado galloped toward the subway; it was nearing five and the rush was on. After a quick phone call, Abel miraculously corralled a cab, directing the driver to the Wolberg Brothers brokerage firm on Broad Street.

Sampson joined the mob at one of the station's bars, and bellowed for a drink in such a loud and eerie voice that the stunned bartender served him at once. Feeling much better, he pushed out into the rush-hour surge. Lulled by the familiar

49

and oblivious to the decibellic fury which raged about him, Sampson scuffed his way along 42nd Street, heading for home and Savvy. Passing Times Square, his glance wandered into a grimy window, one of those bookstores that specialize in a combination of exotica and erotica. "YOUR HANDWRITING IS YOUR FUTURE," screamed lurid red letters. And he stopped. Two men promptly bumped into him from behind, mouthing words he didn't have to read.

He stared at the dirty window with its horde of fly corpses, not really seeing them, but recalling the personal effects of Harrison Wolberg. In his mind, he replayed the succession of items which had been passed to him by Claire Fletcher. He was struck by one particular fact. Nothing in Wolberg's handwriting was left in the notebooks or in his card case. There were none of the scribbled notes which usually litter a man's pockets and wallet. Nothing. Sampson was reasonably sure that Fletcher had not removed anything.

Wondering what that might possibly mean, he quickened his pace.

FOUR

Sampson Trehune looked at himself in the mirror and was pleased. Earlier, while doing his Morning Stoutness Exercises, the pleasure had been considerably less. Now, attired in his best suit, a gray single-breasted job with belted back, and a yellow-toned wide paisley tie which complemented his dark brown eyes—or, at least, so Sadie said—he had to admit he looked rather handsome. For forty-four.

As he picked a bit of lint from his right sleeve, he thought of Harry the tailor, who was deaf. Harry was expensive, but worth it. A craftsman, he insisted on cutting Sampson's jacket to a size 38 pattern and making slight alterations during the fitting. Sampson had been a size 38 since he hit the middle-age slump in his late thirties.

Harry also had a great sense of humor. During a fitting, he always entertained Sampson with a fund of stories extolling the wisdom of the deaf and highlighting the idiocy of Hearers. While his chalk, needle, and scissors darted about Sampson's middle, Harry would sign his stories with one hand, frequently using the fitting mirror for the punchline. "So this old lady says to me, 'Ah, you're deaf, are you?' and I nod and continue spelling to Artie—you remember Artie, the deaf watchmaker over on 77th?—and she watches for a while, then chimes in, 'Fascinating, just fascinating. I have always wanted to learn Braille.'"

Sampson opened his bureau drawer and took out a battered tin cigar case. Inside were several large black buttons of varying sizes and styles. His hand hovered over the open tin, hesitated, and finally selected a large, smooth plastic button. Walking to the mirror, he deftly inserted the button into his left ear, and smiled approval. The button was the perfect touch.

On several occasions in the past, Sampson had wished to emphasize the fact that he was deaf, or at least give the impression that he was hard of hearing. At the sight of a button in his ear, Hearers would suddenly turn considerate and speak slowly and distinctly in front of his face, so he could see what they were saying. Of course they were shouting, but that bothered Sampson not a bit. If the Hearers would speak so he could see them, and they had to strain their voices to do it, that was their tough luck. Sometimes he even added a bit of black wire wending from his ear to his breast pocket, but with the advent of micro-circuitry, he rarely found that necessary. "All transistorized," he would explain when Hearers asked where the wires were. "Self-contained, just like the moon rocket." This always impressed Hearers. Their eyes fixed on the button, they never realized that Sampson was reading their speech. Hearers were like that.

He checked his pocket to make sure he had the business card that Harrison Wolberg had given him at their first meeting. It had taken him half an hour to find it in his desk junk drawer. He set the alarm and, near his apartment, jumped a cab to the brokerage house on Broad Street.

Sampson was charmed when he entered the firm's large, high-ceilinged public room. He stood for several moments absorbing it. He couldn't hear, of course, but he knew that the room was cool and hushed. A sacred place. À la Proust, he was instantly transported to his childhood when, staying with his mother at her New Surrey home, he had frequently visited Edington Cathedral, a fourteenth-century Benedictine church.

The moment passed, but the comparison stayed. Opposite the door at the first of a row of desks along the far wall sat a broker, his hands folded. Lips pursed in priestly fashion, he nodded sagely to a client seated across from him. The man had a face just made for foreclosing mortgages, evicting widows and orphans, and refusing life-or-death pleas from the needy.

Behind him were lined eight more desks, each occupied by a priest in a dark-colored conservative suit, each occupant gazing toward the altar, where orange symbols and figures moved rapidly across the twin market boards. Beyond were the private offices, corresponding to the monks' cells, where daily meditations were conducted for the salvation of themselves and other worshipers.

The worshipers sat in rows of straight-backed, uncomfortable wooden chairs, separated from the rest of the church by a wooden rail. As Sampson watched, one of the acolytes or lesser clerics took a strip of paper from an ancient ticker tape, approached the pulpit in the far corner, and studiously read aloud some news of tremendous import to the congregation.

Sampson chuckled silently, and felt a slight tug at his sleeve, at which he turned.

A man was saying to him, "You seem pleased by the news about Intex. Did you have a short sale? I don't believe we've met." The man, well dressed, well scrubbed, was talking directly at the button in Sampson's ear. Quickly, Sampson gave him one of his cards. "Mr. Trehune. Yes. I'm Joe Welch. Haven't seen you in here before, have we?" In response, Sampson handed Wolberg's card to him. "Yes, I see. Just one moment, please." He disappeared into one of the private offices.

He returned shortly, obviously hurt by an answer he had received. "Mr. McPhee is handling all of Harrison's accounts," he said; "if you will just step this way." Sampson saw that several heads were raised from their desks and looking in their direction. Judging from the strain visible in the man's throat muscles and the way he mouthed his words, he was talking loudly, an irregularity upsetting to worshipers and clergy alike.

McPhee, Sampson discovered, was ancient. He had been with the Wolberg concern since before the great crash and was one of the few customers' men who had survived. His stock and bond recommendations had actually made a bundle for his clients, since he alone among the firm's employees had predicted a bear market. In fact, since 1924, when he had graduated from Princeton and joined the Wolberg firm, then run by the long-deceased Wolberg Senior, he had always predicted a bear market, and worse.

53

"They call it a technical correction," McPhee offered, un-asked, when they were introduced. "But there are serious times ahead, let me tell you. Serious times." He was a small problem for Sampson. His jaw hung slack when he spoke, revealing little lip movement, as if speech were almost too difficult. Gradually, Sampson learned that the conservatism and caution of McPhee were typical of the entire Wolberg Brothers firm. Finally, interrupting yet another forecast of a falling market, Sampson got McPhee around to the subject he wanted to discuss.

"New issues," McPhee said, raising his eyebrows and mar-shaling his most telling predictions. "Red herrings?" shaking his head sadly. "Yes, the firm does occasionally underwrite such things. Not that I entirely approve such a use of capital, but Harrison—rest his soul . . . You did know about Harri-son? Dead. Some miracle cure he was experimenting with. Should have gone to my doctor. Best man in the business—just look at me. Well, Harrison did occasionally involve the firm in new-issue underwriting. If you are sure . . ." He looked sadly at Sampson, shuffled away into an inner office, and returned, his arms filled with folders.

"Let me see." He rummaged, and produced a list of forth-coming issues which the Wolberg firm was either wholly or partially underwriting, some eight firms in all. The second name on the list was Bannon Electronics, Inc. "Bannon? Yes, yes, seems a safe issue. His wife, you know. Her father, Senator Ellis. Rumor has it that the company is in line for some new government contracts. Needed expansion. Let me see," more rummaging, and another trip to the inner office. Sampson was given a prospectus on the new issue of Bannon Electronics stock.

"Not too many of these left; seems the issue is popular, oversubscribed. Then, too, quite small public offering, only a hundred thousand shares. In fact, can't guarantee you'll be able to get in. But if you'll leave me your name and number, Mr.—aaahh," He fumbled, and Sampson tactfully presented the brown-spotted hand with another business card. "Ah, yes, Mr. Trehune. Well, I'm handling Harrison's portfolios, so I'll see what I can do for you. Yes."

Sampson stuffed the material into his inner pocket and was about to leave when the door of a private office opened. Claire Fletcher, accompanied by two men, walked slowly into the main office.

"That's Mr. Morton Bannon," offered McPhee, indicating one of the men, "principal shareholder, Bannon Electronics. This is his first move to go public and . . ."

Sampson turned to find Claire Fletcher staring at him, wide-eyed. She left the two men and strode over to him. "Well, well, Mr. Trehune. I wouldn't have thought you played the market. Or are you looking for something else?" Sampson ignored her question. Bannon joined them and was introduced, painfully, by McPhee. The man with Bannon, rumpled and unshaven, turned out to be Murray Wolberg, Harrison's younger brother. Wolberg said little, and seemed embarrassed by Sampson's presence. Bannon, on the other hand, was positively voluble. He gestured as he spoke, nodding with his gray crew-cut head, encompassing the office with his arms. "Great time, great time. A very good time to bring out a new issue. The market's ripe—isn't that so, Murray? Economy's in prime health." He continued, getting little encouragement from Murray Wolberg, "It is terrible, though, that the Bannon issue had to be marred by the tragedy of Harrison's death. Terrible." Murray appeared to be wishing he were somewhere else.

After they had said their good-byes, Fletcher lingered a moment and said to Sampson, looking him directly in the face, "Why are you wearing a button in your ear?"

"Hearing aid," said Sampson.

"Shit," she said. Sampson had not learned to read that word until well into his teens. He smiled. She turned briskly and strode off, her stock soaring with the dazzled Sampson.

When he left the Wolberg offices, it was ten minutes past eleven, and McPhee was fiddling with plastic numbers, posting the eleven-o'clock volume on the office board, shaking his head sadly as he did so. Sampson felt grateful to McPhee, for he now had another bit of information. While searching for a prospectus on a new cosmetics firm, McPhee, frustrated, had mentioned to Murray Wolberg that Harrison probably took it out of the office—actually took away their only copy. Murray, conciliatory, assured him that it was most likely in his desk, misfiled or something. McPhee insisted otherwise. "Lately, he's been taking things with him at night—most unusual."

"But that's why he moved into the 2800 Building," Murray had said, "to be close to the office, in town, so he could work. I'll be going over there this afternoon, I'll look. Don't worry."

Jodie, long gone, had lived at a place called the 2800 Building. A hip apartment hotel which specialized in single tenants—a management rule—and no questions asked. Astronomical rent was also a feature. Another building by that name? It seemed a most unlikely spot for Harrison Wolberg to choose as a hideaway in the city where he could retire at night and pore over the Dow-Jones averages. It didn't fit at all.

As Sampson opened the door to his apartment, a folded piece of paper caught his attention, mostly because of Savvy, who was happily chewing on it. Sampson retrieved the crumpled paper and read the neat block lettering on it: TELEPHONE CALL. T.J. had received a call for him. After a quick walk with the dog, Sampson knocked on T.J.'s door. As a concession, he allowed Savvy to accompany him, and the dog was soon romping through T.J.'s apartment.

56

"Doc-tor A-bel called. He said you would prob-ab-ly want to know. The au-top-sy on Har-ri-son Wol-berg. Doc-tor Alt-man called him." Sampson nodded impatiently, but T.J. would not be hurried. "Ab-so-lute-ly noth-ing."

"Nothing?" Sampson barked.

"Well, he had a case of hem-or-rhoids and a t—"

Sampson closed his eyes. Obviously nothing unusual had turned up at Wolberg's autopsy. Obviously Voisin was either mistaken or a fraud. And yet Sampson felt funny about it. Odd. Nothing identifiable, just odd.

T.J. was staring at him. "Well, no mys-ter-y, no ex-cite-ment, huh, Sampson?" T.J. looked positively crestfallen.

Sampson said nothing, but handed him Wolberg's business card, and the Hastings newspaper account of his death. He pointed to the list of names in the article—the doctors', Claire Fletcher's, his own. "Call them; see who has an account there."

"But they won't tell me," T.J. protested.

"Invent. Lie," Sampson offered airily, and immersed himself in the prospectus of Bannon Electronics while his friend struggled with the telephone.

"This offering involves risks!" Sampson was warned on the first page of the Bannon prospectus. "These securities have not been approved or disapproved by the Securities and Exchange Commission nor has the Commission passed upon the accuracy or adequacy of this prospectus. Any representation to the contrary is a criminal offense."

"These securities," he learned, were 200,000 shares of Class A Common Stock (No Par Value), of which 100,000 shares were being retained by the officers of Bannon Electronics and another 100,000 shares were being offered to the public, for purchase at a price of not more than $15 per share.

Bannon Electronics, he read, had two subsidiaries, both of which were purchased within the past five years by an exchange of Bannon stock. The first subsidiary, the Electronetics Corporation, in which Bannon Electronics had a controlling interest, bought material and manufactured components for the parent company's products. Assembly of such products took place at Bannon's Hastings plant. The other company, also acquired by an exchange of Bannon stock, was New England Med-Art, Inc., with home offices in Philadelphia. Med-Art did a thriving business in hospital disposables, its line covering everything from patients' nightgowns to a new line of disposable scalpels which were inexpensive and increasing in popularity.

Impatient, he struggled through pages of words, figures, and graphs dealing with expansion, new government contracts, retirement of long-term indebtedness, future capitalization, position of companies vis-à-vis competitors, employee relations, shareholder voting rights.

He was assured by the prospectus that "the legality of the shares offered hereby is being passed upon by Sterling Newton, of New York, counsel for Bannon Electronics and the underwriters, Wolberg Bros., Inc., of New York."

Any lingering doubts of a prospective investor were dealt with in the final six pages, where he would learn that Bannon Electronics, Inc., had shifted to a system of equity accounting and that three independent accounting firms—Hoven & Neds, J. R. Leonard, and Balaban & Sons—had examined, respectively, the books of Bannon Electronics, the Electronetics Corporation, and New England Med-Art, Inc. "The examination was made in accordance with generally accepted accounting principles. . . . The statements contained in this prospectus present fairly the financial position of Bannon Electronics and its subsidiaries."

It looked like a very good investment indeed.

Sampson also learned that an hour of reading such material gave him a splitting headache. T.J.'s comments didn't help it any.

"Well, I got what you want-ed. On-ly Doc-tor A-bel has an ac-count at Wol-berg's." Sampson scowled and clapped his hands, which brought Savvy hurrying to his side.

"Thanks anyway," he said, and returned to his own apart-ment.

Ten minutes later he was back. "Call the Altman Clinic, in Hastings. Speak to purchasing agent. Be salesman. Get ap-pointment. Represent new line of hospital products. Dis-posables. Real cheap."

It took half an hour, but T.J. finally put down the receiver and shook his head sadly. "No luck. I did-n't talk to the pur-chas-ing a-gent. They don't have an-y. Doc-tor Alt-man does most of the buy-ing for the cli-nic."

"So?"

"Well, his sec-re-tar-y said it would-n't do any good to drive out and see him. The cli-nic uses New Eng-land Med-Art sup-plies ex-clu-sive-ly."

"There may be something in what you say, Rabbit. I must move about more. I must come and go." Sampson went, leav-ing T.J. in a state of confusion, a not infrequent result of his friend's visits.

FIVE

"No, stupid, it's not your brother—it's a real dummy!" The name on the mailbox and the metal tag pinned to his dirty olive-drab shirt identified the speaker as Francis Xavier Rizzo, superintendent of the 2800 Building. Two flights down was his wife. The dummy in question was Sampson himself, who fumed inwardly as he watched one side of the shouting match.

Sampson thought of the deaf Beethoven who had mastered his handicap to produce the Ninth Symphony. Although Sampson had never heard it, friends assured him it was Beethoven's finest achievement. He fought down an impulse to shove the super over the railing.

Rizzo paused, listening, then added to his invisible antagonist, "Oh, yeah! Well, it's sure as hell funny that your brother's never around when there's any work to be done!" He faced Sampson squarely, mouthing, "Women, all the time women." Rizzo's face softened to something like sympathy as he returned to the problem which Sampson's presence had created. Sampson tried to look pitiful.

If asked precisely what he was doing prowling around the 2800 Building on that Tuesday afternoon when he was caught by Rizzo, Sampson would have shrugged and said, "Just curious." His friend Abel had a much more complicated explanation with which, from time to time, he belabored Sampson.

"You see, you feel cut off, isolated from normal human communication because of your deafness. Hence, you are not merely curious—not in the normal sense. No, you suffer from a positive obsession to snoop—I am using layman's language now, of course—yes, to snoop. Things which you do not understand actually offend you—or, more accurately perhaps, frighten you. You feel compelled to poke about until you are satisfied in your own mind. . . ."

An hour earlier, Sampson had been sitting in his apartment feeling a bit isolated. He had not consciously decided to go snooping; he had simply decided to become anonymous and go for a walk. He had long ago perfected a special way of being invisible. He had dressed in an old jacket, raising false hopes in Savvy, who anticipated a romp through a nearby park. Instead, Sampson had picked up a tattered cardboard sheet, at the top of which was printed, "THE PERSON WHO HANDS YOU THIS CARD IS DEAF." The rest of the sheet was filled with shameless pleas for charity. He had pocketed a couple of playing-card copies of the deaf finger alphabet and set off on a walk down Seventh Avenue in the general direction of the 2800 Building.

Rizzo now placed a grimy paw on Sampson's shoulder, and confided, "Yeah, fellah, I know things are tough for you people. Things are tough all over, believe me. But I can't let you panhandle in this here building. I mean, we got some class tenants, lots of young people, real swingers—know what I mean?—and they don' wanna be bothered." Sampson looked properly forlorn.

"Tell ya what, though . . . If you wanna make a few bucks an' help me out . . ." Sampson nodded eagerly, wondering what Rizzo had in mind. The man beckoned, and Sampson followed him up to the fourth floor, then down a hallway. Rizzo stopped in front of a door. In the dim light, Sampson could make out the name above the brass knocker: "WOLBERG." "This guy was killed," volunteered Rizzo. "Gotta get his stuff moved out. Empty apartments don't bring the agency no money, and anyway his brother's coming by to collect the stuff soon."

The two men entered the apartment. "This here's a furnished place, so we don't gotta move no furniture or any big stuff; just pack what I point to, O.K.?" Sampson nodded. "You know, you read lips real good," Rizzo acknowledged. Sampson shuffled faintly and looked down.

There were half a dozen empty cardboard boxes already in the apartment, in anticipation of the packing and removal of the contents of drawers, closets, and table tops. Sampson saw Rizzo scoop a handful of loose change from the bureau into his pocket, then settle down to leaf through a stack of men's magazines, the kind with large, glossy centerfolds.

Nearly finished, Sampson picked up the blotter from the desk, and laid it atop the last box. Rizzo had abandoned the

61

magazines and was adding jackets and ties to a pile of clothing laid out on the bed; his broad back was turned away.

It fell out from underneath the blotter, and Sampson almost put it into the box without looking. There were two items clipped together: a picture, the sort night clubs offer their customers as a remembrance of things past. In it, Harrison Wolberg˙ was smiling shyly at a strikingly beautiful young woman, blond and well built, in a low-cut evening dress. Attached to it was a bank deposit slip, with the name "Jennifer Reed" imprinted. The deposit was dated a month before, in the amount of five hundred dollars. It was simply listed as "modeling fee," followed by a bank number 60-12/211. Sampson studied it for a moment. Then he slipped the two items into his pocket and began a diligent search of the rest of the room. He moved quickly, earning an appreciative nod from Rizzo for his thoroughness.

He found only a few matchbooks from a bar in the Wall Street area; the Ticker Tap it was called. He pocketed one, and looked up to find Rizzo glaring at him.

"Whatcha got there, huh? Come on, I don' want no stealin' goin' on. Give you guys a break, 'n' waddya do? Cheez." Sampson, hangdog, brought out the book of matches. "Aw, that's O.K. Keep 'em," said Rizzo generously. He picked up an armload of clothing and headed out the door. In a minute, he was back looking angry. "I said pick up a box and come on. What's a matter, are you—" He caught himself. "Oh, yeah, I forgot. You *are* deaf, ain't you? Well, grab a box and follow me." He pantomimed the gestures. Sampson picked up a box and waited while Rizzo closed but did not lock the door. "Come on," he ordered, and Sampson trooped after him down the three flights of stairs.

"Go back and get the rest. I'll wait here," said Rizzo, depositing his armload of clothing on one of the lobby chairs. "Door's open."

62

Sampson climbed the stairs, legs aching, head and heart pounding as he neared the top. In the hallway, winded from the climb, he leaned for a moment against the wall and inhaled deeply. Rizzo, although not smoking, carried with him an aura of cheap cigars. His absence seemed to clear the air, and Sampson, once inside the room, became aware of a slight sweetness—perfume, perhaps. Not men's shaving lotion —too strong for that.

Idly he poked through a box into one end of which Rizzo had swept the contents of the medicine cabinet. It didn't require the shade of Sherlock Holmes to come to a quick conclusion: two toothbrushes, neither new; two brands of toothpaste; three bars of soap, each a different color and shape, each expensive; a styptic pencil; three pairs of tweezers; two razors, one large and masculine, the other small in a pink leather case; and so forth. Rummaging in another box, he came upon an unopened package containing three pairs of nylon panty hose. Quickly he looked at the picture. Gauging her height and general build, he found the nylons corresponded. Their color was smoky, a light charcoal. Yes, she seemed the type.

The carton also contained six scrapbooks, cheap with bright pasteboard covers. Three red, one tan, two blue. They had been purchased and used at different times, judging by their rather tattered appearance, and had been filled by Wolberg over several years. Their cheapness was in sharp contrast, Sampson noted, to the expensive tastes of Harrison Wolberg. Left over from his youth? More likely a secret passion he had nurtured in private, meant for no other eyes but his own. Sampson plunged into the first scrapbook and found its pages crowded with neatly clipped and pasted accounts of Nazi war crimes. They had been cut from newspapers and magazines, with their dates starting nearly two decades before. From time to time, a note had been scribbled in the margin with a date, forming a cross-reference system, he soon discovered, to the other scrapbooks.

Then he noticed a pattern to these apparently random clippings. There were very few of the "big names" in these particular accounts. When Rudolf Hess, Goebbels, or Himmler was mentioned, there was invariably another name underscored in the text of the article—usually a doctor's name. The articles were all concerned with the apprehension and prosecution of physicians who had collaborated with the Nazi regime, who had engaged in medical experiments upon prisoners. Jews and gypsies. In the camps or in so-called medical research centers, both in Germany and in the occupied countries.

He became so engrossed in what he was reading that he didn't feel the usual warning tingle at the back of his neck that told him of a presence behind him. When he turned and looked up from his kneeling position, Rizzo was standing there, red in the face and flapping his mouth furiously. Sampson caught a few of the words: ". . . damn, your kind, just like all the rest of the bums. You people don' wanna work, just a free handout, somethin' for nothin', that's all. Even when somebody gives you a chance t'earn an honest dollar, whaddya do? Jus' sit on yer ass and goof off. Yer all alike."

Apparently the violent start which Sampson had registered at the unexpected appearance of the super had been interpreted as plain, cowering fear. Pretty soon, Rizzo wore down. "Cheez, fellah, you think I got all day? Now damn it, come on, the car's waitin' to pick these things up. Big Caddie, lotsa class, an' he won't wanna be kept waitin'." Trapped, Sampson obediently lifted a box under each arm and followed Rizzo down the stairs to the lobby, and back up again alone for a final load.

Halfway down the last flight of stairs, Sampson halted suddenly, pretending to shift his grip on the boxes. Murray Wolberg was just leaving the lobby with an armload of clothes. Beyond, through the glass doors, nestled by the curb, sat a sleek maroon Fleetwood. The back door was open, and Rizzo was reverently depositing his burden on the back seat. He turned and relieved Murray Wolberg of the clothes he was carrying, and laid them on the seat also. In front Sampson could discern the unmistakable profile of Claire Fletcher, gazing coolly forward, not bothering to turn her head to observe this mundane piece of business.

Sampson went quickly down the remaining stairs, deposited the boxes, and ducked out of sight just as the two men returned to the lobby. Rizzo scanned the room and shook his head, mouth working. Murray just nodded, picked up two cartons, and carried them to the waiting car. The super followed, arms waving, mouth moving as though chomping on an invisible carrot. After the last load, Wolberg took out his wallet, extracted several bills, and closed Rizzo's hand over them. Still talking, Rizzo carelessly waved one hand while inspecting the money clutched in the other.

Sampson counted to sixty and then emerged from his hiding place. "Where the hell were you when I needed you?" Rizzo said. Sampson tried to sign that he had gone upstairs for another load. "But we already got the last box. Boy, are you dumb. You know, I really shouldn't give you nothin' for goofin' off so much. But here. Take it and get out." Super Rizzo reached into his pocket and handed Sampson the change which he had taken from Wolberg's dresser. Sampson took it, twisting his face into a grimace of gratitude, and bowed as Rizzo held open the lobby door for him.

As he shuffled past, he brought his foot down hard on Rizzo's left instep. Over his shoulder, Sampson saw pain curl the super's face. Nice. "Sorry," said Sampson.

He hailed a cab and handed the driver the Ticker Tap matchbook. Halfway there, he remembered that he was dressed in far too lowly a fashion for his purpose. He took out one of his cards and indicated the address on Twenty-ninth Street to the obviously suspicious driver. In front of his apartment, Sampson jumped out of the cab, told the driver to wait, and paid him the meter fare and a tip. "Wait," he repeated.

In the apartment, he found Savvy indignantly waiting to go out. He snapped on the leash and escorted the dog downstairs and along the length of the block, passing the astonished cabdriver, who shrugged comically and relapsed into the seat.

Back in the apartment, Sampson settled the mollified Savvy, changed back into his gray suit, and popped the black button into his ear, and within minutes he was speeding toward the money capital of the world. He pondered a remark Claire Fletcher had made on Monday—God, that was only yesterday?—while they were speculating on the possible reasons for Wolberg's murder. "If it ain't love, it's money," she pronounced. Once again, Sampson was puzzled and vaguely uneasy; her remark had seemed so snappy and flip. Sampson liked things as tidy as anyone else, but still . . . Love or money. Did the one exclude the other?

Even though the Ticker Tap had a Wall Street address, it was much too far from the center of activity for secretaries and junior executives to pop over for an hour's lunch. The interior was a hapless blend of English pub and New York nightery. The windows facing the street were stained glass, sporting red, purple, and yellow peacocks. Watneys Red Barrel was served in tall frosted mugs, and a dartboard, much used, occupied a prominent place against a wall. There were no stools at the bar, and apparently women were discouraged, if not barred, from the taproom. Beyond, clearly visible, was a dining room, smart, sparkling, and slick.

A few well-dressed men were scattered at the low tables in the taproom, and two of them were talking with the bartender as he polished glasses and sliced lemons with a deft, easy authority. He broke off the conversation to move over to the new customer, bringing a clean cloth with him to wipe the already spotless bar while he asked the customer's preference. Sampson indicated the plastic red barrel and nodded. Expertly, the man drew a frothy dark brew and placed the mug on the counter top. He picked up a five-dollar bill, returned three singles, and was about to leave when Sampson stopped him.

He pointed elaborately to his watch, which now read 4:18. He pointed to the button in his ear, and then to his lips, shaking his head. The bartender was puzzled. "Wolberg," Sampson said, in his most careful voice. "Drink at four. Late." And he gestured around the room. Then he produced Harrison Wolberg's business card and laid it on the bar.

The bartender stared at the card for a moment, and looked up helplessly at Sampson, who then placed the photograph of Wolberg and the stacked blonde in front of him. "Wolberg. Four o'clock. Some stocks. Drink," he recited, giving the man time. Now recognition dawned on the bartender's face. He raised his hand, indicating he would be back momentarily, and walked to the end of the bar where he spoke to the two men. They looked at Sampson and shook their heads. The bartender nodded, reached under the bar, and returned to Sampson, carrying a newspaper. It was folded to an abbreviated account of the death by heart failure of Harrison Wolberg while visiting in Hastings, Connecticut. "Sunday last. Sorry." Sampson registered shock, then waited while the bartender looked soulful and said what a shame it was, but that death comes finally to all men, and if it had to happen, maybe better this way, quick. . . .

Sampson nodded, drained his mug, ordered another. When it was served, he paid for it and pointed to the picture again, indicating the young woman with Wolberg.

67

"Jenny?" The man thought for a moment. "No, come to think of it, I haven't seen her, either, in nearly two weeks. Sorry. But you might try her agency." He left to serve three men who had opened their briefcases and were spreading papers over a table, resuming an animated discussion about something to do with pork bellies. Sampson finished his beer and left, leaving the last single on the bar.

The traffic was miserable, despite the unflinching nerve of his cabdriver, and it was after six when he arrived home. Not stopping to change, he took the stairs two at a time and pounded on T.J.'s apartment door. It was opened immediately by T.J., who was apparently about to leave. He was dressed in a modish suit, maroon and dark pink, with a tie that blossomed down his front and hurt Sampson's eyes. And he was reeking of aftershave.

Sampson entered, closed the door, sighed, and shook his head. "She's going to have to wait. You can be a few minutes late." It wasn't a question, and it was T.J.'s turn to look sad and forlorn.

"Well, all right. But Ger-al-dine does-n't like—" Sampson waved the rest to silence and handed him the matchbook with the Ticker Tap's number and address. "Call. Tell them you're an accountant. At Wolberg's. Working late. Trying to settle Harrison Wolberg's bills. See if he owes them any money. Be convincing." He paced and fidgeted while T.J. dialed and talked for what seemed a rather long time. Finally, T.J. put down the receiver and turned to Sampson. "An-oth-er num-ber," he said. Sampson fumed. More dialing and more talking which he couldn't see.

"Got it!" T.J. announced proudly, and handed Sampson a pad he had been jotting on. For September, Harrison Wolberg had an unpaid balance of $641. In addition, a hundred dollars had been totted up in the early days of October. Sampson stared at the figures, closed his eyes, and waited. Nothing.

No inspiration. No urge to spring up, grab T.J. by the arm, and say something fraught with significance—something like, "Hurry, old fellow, the game's afoot."

"Some-thing else. The own-er, name of Bar-ton, was hap-py I called. Wor-ried a-bout his mon-ey. Read of Wol-berg's death. He al-ways paid prompt-ly, by the tenth. Did-n't pay this month."

Sampson stared. "Bar-ton asked if Jen-ni-fer Reed was al-lowed to con-tin-ue on Har-ri-son's ac-count. I said no, since I did-n't know. . . . What? Wait a minute. What game? Whose foot? Where are we going?"

The cab stopped in front of a restaurant on Forty-sixth Street, where T.J. collected Geraldine. She was tall, a full head taller than T.J. Probably much of their courtship was conducted over the telephone where she could be melted by T.J.'s voice. Geraldine was not amused: "We'll miss dinner, or the seven-fifty feature, or both." She sat rigidly beside the driver, and waited firmly in the cab while Sampson and T.J., armed with a name and a photograph, made the rounds of the agencies where a model might have her name on file for work.

Despite the fact that it was well beyond normal office hours, a surprising number of agencies were still open. "It's a strange bus-i-ness," T.J. observed to no one in particular. "Not nor-mal at all." Sampson nodded.

Less than an hour later, Sampson was seated in the paneled waiting room of an agency specializing in hostesses. T.J. re-turned from an inner office where he had spent the last ten minutes, and handed Sampson the original picture of Harri-son Wolberg and his blond friend. He also held an applica-tion form and four eight-by-ten glossy photographs, com-posites featuring a young woman in a variety of poses, ranging from the prim to the nearly pornographic. It was Wolberg's companion, beyond any doubt. The name on the application form was Jennifer Reed.

"You can keep them. The a-gen-cy nev-er placed her, and she has-n't been back in months. Pret-ty fa-ces are a dime a doz-en."

The cab deposited T.J. and Geraldine in front of Mon Maison, for a dinner compliments of Sampson Trehune, and sped back to Twenty-ninth Street. With a sigh, Sampson locked the door of his apartment, spied the truculent Savvy, and unlocked the door again. "Bother," he signed to the dog, who proceeded haughtily past him toward his leash. "That's right, I said, 'Bother.' You hear me?"

Finally, he settled down to reread the application form. The statistics were average, at least for a model: 5'9", 36-26-36, 128 lbs., silver blond, dark blue, no scars. But near the bottom of the page he read, "PLACE OF BIRTH: Hastings, Conn."

On the reverse, in the box labeled "PROFESSIONAL EXPERI-ENCE," he noted that a year ago Jennifer Reed had worked as a hostess at the annual convention of the American Hospital Association in Atlanta. She had spent three days dressing up the display booth of New England Med-Art, Inc.

SIX

Like a child's fingers fumbling with his first puzzle, Sampson's mind groped among the events of the past three days. Nothing fitted; the pieces refused to form even a part of any design. Tuesday night passed into Wednesday morning without progress. He kept returning to one question in particular: what, specifically, had Voisin meant last Sunday when he said,

"There are points on the human body where even a slight needle puncture can cause serious harm, even death"? Sampson fidgeted, scanned Voisin's book, but found no mention of such points.

Still, Voisin's cryptic remark sparked a dim light in a corner of his memory. Finally, there was nothing to do but check through his entire collection of books on needle therapy. Early Wednesday morning, he discovered what he had been looking for in a rare first edition. It was written by Pol Darby, entitled *La Médecine Chez les Chinois*, and published in Paris by Henri Plon in 1863. Darby combined the French passion for analysis and detail with their equal passion for the exotic and macabre. In a chapter noted more for its mystery than clarity, Sampson found an oblique reference—based, the author admitted, on hearsay—to *la piqûre morte*, the death prick.

He went to bed at 4 A.M., after taking Savvy for a brief walk, and slept happily until nearly ten the next morning.

His elation left him over his second cup of coffee. He really wasn't any closer to a satisfactory understanding of Wolberg's death or, especially, the reliability and safety of acupuncture. What he wanted was to talk to an acupuncturist who was not involved in the Hastings affair, to get an unbiased opinion on a few questions which he had typed and which now stared up at him from the kitchen table. But finding an acupuncturist, biased or not, even in a city the size of New York was not easy. Just for the hell of it, he looked in the Yellow Pages but found that they blithely skipped from Actuaries to Adding Machines & Supplies, with not even a cross-reference for acupuncture.

He would have to smell one out—quite literally. Not a far-fetched idea. He knew that most acupuncturists practicing in New York are Chinese; their offices are usually located behind a combination herb shop, vegetable mart, and drugstore in Chinatown. He knew also that many acupuncturists practice moxabustion; in this procedure, a mound of burning mugwort is placed over a point that has been needled to allow heat to penetrate the affected area.

Burning mugwort has an odor unlike anything else, a combination, so descriptions agreed, of frankincense and wet, smoldering leaves. Although he couldn't recall ever experiencing such an odor, Sampson was confident he would recognize it. "I may not hear, but I smell good," he often bragged.

When Sampson stepped through the door of Sheng's Herb Shop, the seventh he had been in that day, he inhaled deeply and smiled. He smelled what he was searching for. In the previous shops, his questions had elicited no response except fright, probably caused by his strange voice. And he had sensed no telltale signs. Now, among a mixture of odors, one dominated, permeating the whole shop. Sampson inhaled again, enjoying the new sensation—pleasant, appealing, haunting. In the back room, he was sure, was a man with needles.

Sheng's was located in a winding cul-de-sac just off Mott Street, sandwiched between a small Chinese restaurant and an even smaller, vacant storefront. Only one customer was in the shop, an elderly Chinese gentleman, dressed from round cap to manicured shoes in traditional black. As the gentleman discussed his purchases with the squat, middle-aged clerk behind the counter, Sampson explored, happy to be left alone for a few moments.

Sampson could, from past experience, identify a few of the shop's wares. When Abel had first become interested in acupuncture, he was convinced that the cures attributed to the needles resulted partially from the ingestion, perhaps unwitting, of therapeutic drugs. He had hauled Sampson along on investigatory trips through the Chinese shops.

"What's this?" Abel had persistently asked, with maddening Western thoroughness. "Amazing," he said to one explanation. "Simple foxglove. The medical profession recently applauded the discovery of digitalis without recognizing that the Chinese have been using it for centuries in the form of foxglove. Which proves . . ." Sampson had turned away from the lecture, and picked up a handful of small, round globes, grayish-black in color and quite hard. He later learned that they were the dried testicles of arctic seals. Despite his continuing curiosity about textures and densities, he had touched very few items after that.

Sheng's shop was apparently prosperous. A large selection of meat was displayed in an unrefrigerated glass case to the right of the counter. Above the case a dressed duck hung from a flickering neon light, one of the few modern anomalies in the shop, which also had a shiny new scale, a motley collection of canned goods imported from Taiwan, and a dozen cellophane packages of noodles. Otherwise, the shop might have existed in China two thousand years ago.

More strings, suspended from ceiling pipes or tacked to the dingy green walls, ended in other traditional Chinese medicines which Sampson identified as cicada skins, dried toads, and split lizards. On the top shelf behind the counter he even recognized a mound of brownish-black ovals—bear bladders, which he'd been told were an effective but expensive cure for rheumatism. Lower shelves held animal claws, bones, and a variety of dried bits and pieces. To the left of the counter were three large brown sacks of rice, opened to display their contents. Behind them were rows of jars. Sampson moved closer to examine and sometimes sniff small wicker baskets containing a complete range of medicinal herbs: cardamom, cinnamon, tarragon, dried dandelions, ginger, nutmeg, the bark of pomegranate trees, tiny asparagus stalks, and bamboo shoots. Next to these were small trays with ready-mixed powders, granules, pastes, and other assorted curatives, none of which he recognized.

A tug at his left sleeve interrupted his explorations. He turned to find the clerk smiling, bobbing his head, and mouthing something Sampson could not understand. He decided he'd better buy something, and, with the clerk at his elbow, he pointed to a small ginseng root. In powdered form it is a useful, mild sedative. It is worn whole by Chinese gentlemen as an amulet guaranteed to ward off disease and attract women. Why not? thought Sampson.

The oddly shaped root was carefully weighed and ceremoniously wrapped in white tissue paper. After several ineffectual attempts at dialogue, the clerk finally wrote out the price: $12. Sampson recalled that ginseng sold for $250 a pound. Oh, well. He paid to the accompaniment of bows, smiles, and, no doubt, wishes for immediate good fortune.

"Doctor here?" Sampson asked.

"Good, all very good," said the clerk, ignoring Sampson's question. Did he really not understand or was he pretending?

"Doctor," repeated Sampson, and took out one of his business cards. "CH'I," he printed, Chinese for the life force which flows along the meridians of acupuncture.

The clerk looked at the card and was visibly shaken. Head jerking from left to right, his mouth a study in perpetual motion, the man made it impossible for Sampson to understand him.

Impulsively, Sampson headed toward the back-room door, but the clerk got there before him, moving around the counter with surprising speed. He blocked Sampson's path and menaced him with a knife plucked from the butcher's block behind the counter. Sampson couldn't tell whether anger or fear had the upper hand. He didn't really care. Simultaneously, his stomach and feet sent out a message: "Bear of Little Brain, get out of here."

The tableau was interrupted by a young Chinese, dressed in a Western suit, who emerged from the back room. Calmly he spoke to the clerk, whose expression changed. After a bow and an embarrassed glance at the knife, the clerk returned quickly to his position behind the counter.

The newcomer studied Sampson thoroughly, then said, "You are deaf." Sampson read no question mark in his eyes.

Sampson nodded.

"Come," the man said, and led him into the rear of the shop. "Wait, please." He gestured toward a chair.

Sampson sat down and watched the man cross the room to stand beside a table fitted with a thin mattress. On it was a Chinese man, who nodded when the first man, apparently the doctor, returned and said something Sampson couldn't see. The doctor picked up a soupçon of mugwort from a small silver tray next to the table. He rolled it between his fingers, compressing it into a delicate miniature cone. He placed the herb cone over a point on the man's shoulder, struck a match at least six inches long, and lit the leaves. A wisp of smoke rose and quickly dissipated, and a wave of sweetness filled the room.

The doctor held the patient's wrist, reading the pulses of acupuncture. He nodded, removed the still-burning cone, and replaced it with another which was lit and burned in the same fashion. The process was repeated a third time before the doctor seemed satisfied. He waved the patient off into a cubicle masked by a bamboo curtain. Time to rest.

The doctor sat down behind his desk, facing Sampson. On the wall to his left were the customary charts, life-size, of the meridians of acupuncture, with the points indicated by Chinese characters. An ivory doll or statue of a man occupied the desk space that Westerners would reserve for family photographs. The meridians were sketched almost imperceptibly in blue, the points in red characters. Lifting a ceramic pot from a hot plate on a table beside him, the doctor poured two cups of tea.

"I must apologize for my clerk, Mr.—?"

"Trehune," Sampson said in his best voice, and handed the doctor one of his business cards. In turn, the doctor handed Sampson a card. "Chiao Lin-Chuang," it said, followed by several Chinese characters; at the bottom, in English, "Sheng's Herb Shop."

"As I said, Mr. Trehune, you must excuse Yang Joe. Westerners rarely visit us, except the police. Or, more accurately, the New York Board of Education and their special police. I am sure you know that acupuncture is not recognized as a legitimate medical practice. We are continually in danger of being closed down. Just a month ago, some special police broke into a colleague's shop. He followed the old custom of allowing his fingernails to grow. A seventy-six-year-old man with three-inch daggers—a terrifying sight, no doubt. So they struck him. Of course, we're the barbarians."

"I'm not with police," Sampson said.

"I know. It wouldn't matter if you were."

"Why?"

"When a sick person presents himself here, it is my obligation to help him, regardless of who he might be."

More silence, more tea.

"You have been deaf for some time, probably since childhood," said Chiao. "A fever of some sort, then deafness strikes."

Sampson nodded.

"So. You have heard of the supposed miracles that needle therapy works in China, causing the deaf to hear. Now you want to try. I'm afraid that it isn't quite that simple, Mr. Trehune. I must first examine you, a lengthy process. I already have several patients scheduled for this week—"

Sampson interrupted with a wave of his hand. From his

inside jacket pocket he withdrew a brief, if lurid, newspaper account of Harrison Wolberg's death at the acupuncture session in Hastings. Dr. Chiao read the account with interest at first, then with growing distaste. Leaning across the desk, he dropped it in front of Sampson.

"So," he said. "You were to be treated by Dr. Voisin. I have heard of him, of course. But this distresses me. It gives Eastern medicine a bad name—a worse name, actually, since most Westerners think we are little better than witch doctors. Nevertheless, if you return—perhaps next week—we will talk." When Sampson shook his head, the doctor was puzzled.

"Some information," Sampson said, withdrawing a second piece of paper from his pocket. He handed it to the doctor, who scanned it, then reread it thoroughly.

"One moment, please." The doctor disappeared behind the curtain to join his patient. Soon both appeared and, without a glance at Sampson, walked through the doorway to the shop.

"This is unusual, very unusual, Mr. Trehune," Chiao said when he returned to his desk. "But I can see no harm in answering some of your questions. First," the doctor's left thumb moved a quarter of the way down Sampson's list, "I sincerely hope you have no intention of trying to treat yourself. It takes an average of six years to train an acupuncturist. An acupuncturist has pricked himself at least ten thousand times, under expert guidance, before he is allowed to touch a patient. No 'how-to' book could—"

"Scratch the surface," said Sampson, and rushed to another question. "Where does a doctor get needles?"

"Well, it's no great secret, I suppose. Actually, anyone with a bit of tenacity can find out. There are three sources in the world for first-rate needles like these."

Sampson stared in fascination, abruptly bumped back to Sunday night when Wolberg was on the table.

"Taiwan, China, and France," Chiao continued. He twirled

77

a clear plastic tube containing a needle. The base of the needle rested on cotton while the tip was suspended. "Since I am on the East Coast, I have mine supplied by the Trudeau House in Marseilles. They are shipped in gross lots—sterile, ready for use."

"I can buy some?"

"I do not think I would sell you any, Mr. Trehune. Forgive my bluntness. I am sure, though, that with little effort, you could locate a supplier."

More silence, more tea.

"Now, as to your other questions, I am not sure what to say. Yes, it is a demonstrable fact that the pulses can be read after a person has . . . died. If Voisin or any acupuncturist of repute read a cause of death which differed from a typical Western explanation, I would be inclined to agree with him. Yet that would depend on a number of factors. So it is impossible to answer this question without precise details."

Sampson nodded. He had expected as much. East or West, physicians were all the same: no straight answers.

"As to your next questions, I'm afraid I won't discuss them. Again, excuse my rudeness. You ask about—what do you call them?—forbidden points. It's a good enough name, I suppose. Points where an acupuncturist must never puncture or tragedy ensues. I guess I *can* tell you that there are such points on the human body, points which when punctured disturb the flow of Yin and Yang to such a degree that death results.

"But you ask where, Mr. Trehune, and that tempted me to call the police myself. Would you walk into a Western doctor's office, ask him where to buy a scalpel, and then demand specific instructions for a virtually indetectable murder? I think not." Chiao stood up, moved toward the doorway. "No, Mr. Trehune, I would have to know you almost as I know myself before I answered that question."

Recognizing a dismissal that he couldn't fight, Sampson stood up. He took out his wallet.

Chiao, caught between insult and humor, opted for the latter. "I charge, Mr. Trehune, only when I have treated a patient whose pulses show that he is healthier. I do not mean to suggest, of course, that Western doctors have anything to learn from us."

Well, under the circumstances, it passes for humor, thought Sampson while he and Chiao walked to the shop's front door.

"When you have finished this quest of yours, Mr. Trehune, please return. I believe you might be able to hear again." They were standing in the shop's entrance.

"Thank you," said Sampson. Chiao was a Civilized Human Being, reasonable. Or so he thought as he turned to leave. A tap on his shoulder.

"Don't drink so much. It's bad for your liver. In a few years—"

"Bother!" said Sampson.

Out of the cul-de-sac, he walked by shops less prosperous than Sheng's. "Elevenses. Time for a snack," he said to himself, having checked his watch. Not that it was anywhere near that time. It was almost two. The point was he was hungry. He had an Idea. When in Chinatown, he thought, do as the Chinese do. He headed for the Golden Bowl, a favorite restaurant where he knew he could still be served a full menu.

"Planter's Punch," he said carefully, and waved the waiter away. He looked at the menu and then at his watch. This evening, he and Abel were to attend *shivah* at the Wolbergs' and he was supposed to be in Abel's office at six. That settled it. In all probability, there would be no dinner. Better eat well now.

"Duck," he ordered when the waiter returned. "Moo Shi style. One more of these." He waved the soda glass used for

79

an authentic Planter's Punch. Then, since the duck would take nearly an hour to prepare, he added an order of hot hors d'oeuvres, pointing to the appropriate numbers on the menu so the waiter would be sure to understand.

With the aid of another Planter's Punch, Sampson demolished his hors d'oeuvres and was still hungry when his entrée arrived. As he watched the waiter put down the silver dish of folded pancakes stuffed with crisp duck and smothered in a spicy red sauce, then arrange the serving spoons and the teapot, Sampson thought about Chiao. Unlike the waiter's, the doctor's fingers were long, tapered, and extremely facile. He had never moved his hands in a wasted gesture. In fact, the attitude of his whole body had suggested confidence and an unshakable inner repose.

Finished with his meal, Sampson belched contentedly, poured himself a cup of tea, and reviewed the day. He had rediscovered that dedication and belief are contagious. The very confidence of Chiao made it possible for Sampson to accept the existence of pulses after death which an acupuncturist could read. The doctor's refusal to discuss the forbidden points in reality affirmed what Sampson had suspected: that murder *could* be done with a thin acupuncture needle. The doctor had used the word "indetectable."

Sampson left a generous tip, paid the bill, and walked out into the welcome fresh air—as fresh as New York ever provided. The only "hard" fact he had learned today was that anyone could purchase acupuncture needles, no prescription necessary.

He had almost passed a jewelry store when he decided to buy a gold-link bracelet. He asked the jeweler, who chuckled at the request, to drill a hole in his ginseng root and attach it to the bracelet. What the hell, you never know.

Only one recurring thought chafed his good spirits, the result of Planter's Punches, a delectable meal, and renewed faith in acupuncture: if Voisin was right about the efficacy of needle treatment for deafness, he was probably also right about Wolberg's death.

SEVEN

"No, no, no!" T.J. was next to tears. "You will do more harm to the cho-sen peo-ple than all the Ar-ab states combined!"

"Your idea," Sampson said sullenly. Scribbled sheets of paper covered T J.'s kitchen table. Sampson crumpled them into a ball and threw it in the general direction of the wastebasket, missing. He deserted the kitchen for the living room and, flopping into T.J.'s most comfortable chair, acknowledged defeat.

Savvy, whose head hung dejectedly over the edge of T.J.'s sofa, had long since given up. In the first place, with a rap on his rump, Sampson had let him know that the toy dangling from the Boss's wrist was not for him. Sampson had even stuffed the intriguing object out of sight in his pocket. No solace had been offered. No walk. No snack. Not even a pat. Then his ears had been assaulted by the worst sort of human noises. He didn't even lift his head when T.J. sat down beside him.

"I was wrong. I ad-mit," T.J. said to Sampson. "Please, give it up." An hour before, Sampson had stopped by T.J.'s apartment to say that he was going to "Wolberg's wake."

"Well, sit-ting *shi-vah* is not ex-act-ly a wake, Samp-son." Patiently he explained the seven-day ceremony of mourning, the gathering of ten men for the *minyan* at home, the recitation of *Kaddish* by family members, the special candles which are kept burning. But he made one mistake.

"What will I say?" asked Sampson innocently enough.

"Well, to be per-fect-ly pro-per, you should say . . ." And T.J. mouthed something unintelligible.

"What?" asked Sampson, not believing his eyes.

T.J. repeated the strange syllables. "That's He-brew. It means, 'May the Al-might-y com-fort you and all the mourners of Zi-on and Je-ru-sa-lem.'"

Sampson pondered that for a moment, closed his eyes, gathered his strength. He began proudly, in his best voice, "May the Almighty comfort—"

T.J. interrupted, tapping Sampson's hand. "You have to say it in He-brew."

"Teach me," demanded Sampson, the afternoon's Planter's Punches moving him to a degree of hubris he would normally have avoided.

T.J. began, attempting to spell phonetically the Hebrew words; Sampson tried to pronounce them. They made no headway, even though T.J. strove valiantly to find English words which contained sounds equivalent to the Hebrew. Every time Sampson looked directly at T.J.'s face, he read pain.

Now, after a frustrating hour, T.J. sat across from Sampson. "Just say, 'May God com-fort you.' Just that," he suggested. "That's all any-bod-y ex-pects, real-ly. And with your voice, it will sound like you are bro-ken with grief."

Sampson nodded. It must have been bad, for rarely did T.J. comment on the quality of his voice. If only he could hear the words just once, he knew he could say them. If only. A phrase he thought he had forgotten long ago but which had crept back into his thoughts. Foolishness. Sampson rose and left, raising a fist to salute T.J. "*Shalom*," he said, exhausting his supply of Hebrew in one swoop.

Sampson opened the glass door discreetly labeled in gold leaf, "Robert Abel, M.D." It was five after six, but there was no one in the small reception room to note his tardiness. Abel did not employ either a nurse or a secretary, and since his patients were rigidly scheduled, they rarely saw each other.

Leaning back on the tan leather sofa, Sampson glanced despondently at the three tattered magazines on the end table. He had yet to be in Abel's office when a magazine was up-to-date. A step above the magazines was a solitary lamp which, together with a neon tube in the ceiling, provided all the available light. "Singular" was the word for the room: one table, one lamp, one place to sit.

Across the room, opposite the glass door, was a solid wood door with a spring lock. Behind it, Sampson knew, was another door, also locked. The double doors insured that Abel's patients would not be interrupted and that their confessions would not be overheard by anyone in the waiting room. Sampson liked to imagine properly salacious confessions, but Abel never explained what really went on. "We just talk," he said once, "and the patient works out his own problem."

"At fifty an hour," Sampson added.

He and Abel had met nearly a decade before when the good doctor was in his eighth year of practice as a neurosurgeon. At that time, he was wondering how to keep body and soul together, since he averaged only 2.6 neurological operations per year and 8.5 consultations over the same period. Abel had often thought of adding a degree in psychiatry to his neurosurgeon's shingle, but it wasn't until he met Sampson casually at a New York book fair that he had come up with the last word in inspirations.

After browsing through several dealers' stalls, the two had

83

adjourned to a surprisingly uncrowded bar in the Americana Hotel. Sampson swore he had seen dollar signs register in Abel's eyes. Perfect. The deaf, a truly silent minority. Visions of tantalizing neuroses, psychoses, and complexes danced through his head. Abel returned to medical school, underwent an obligatory analysis, and emerged shortly with a second specialty, psychiatry. Then he attended Gallaudet College, in Washington, D.C., taking a crash course as an interpreter-translator for the deaf.

He read everything available on the special problems of the deaf person, and he achieved rare proficiency—for a Hearer—in the finger alphabet and signing. Plugging up his ears, he was even moderately successful at speech-reading; of course, he always had residual hearing to rely on. Marshaling his formidable array of Freudian armaments, he had sat back and waited. Nothing happened. Despite his wide acquaintance with deaf persons, a two-part article on the psychological problems of the deaf, and an appearance on a television talk show devoted to the deaf, no deaf person had ever burdened his analytic couch.

"We're deaf," Sampson would say, dropping his favorite observation, "but not that dumb. Weren't for Hearers, you'd starve."

It was nearing 6:30. Sampson decided to wait another five minutes before pounding on the door of the inner sanctum, the holy of holies. But with one minute to spare, a sprightly young woman, hardly five feet tall despite heels, paraded out of the inner office. She glanced at Sampson, who winked broadly. Startled, she blushed, hesitated, then gave him a smile just as she reached the glass door. When Sampson pulled his eyes away, he encountered Abel framed disapprovingly in the doorway of the inner office.

"I wish you wouldn't disturb my patients," Abel signed.

With reproving bustle, he locked up his office, marched to the elevator, and stabbed a button.

They picked up Abel's car at his garage, a block away, and threaded their way toward Nassau County and the Wolberg family home. Alternately they stopped and started in the last round of the daily battle on the Long Island Expressway. By the time they reached the Westbury exit, Sampson was squirming. He hated traffic; he recognized the automobile as the last word in satanic malice. Besides, he had things to say, questions to ask, but he couldn't talk with Abel. Twilight gloom made it impossible for him to see Abel's face even when the doctor risked facing him.

Sampson made his first faux pas when he was two steps into the Wolberg house. On the first step, following T.J.'s advice and Abel's example, he said in his best voice, "May God comfort you." The eldest Wolberg, Seymour, did not wince at Sampson's voice but reached out to clasp both his arms. To return the embrace, Sampson took his second step forward. His right foot came down on Seymour's unshod left. Sampson had forgotten the family's custom of not wearing shoes during *shivah*. This time, Seymour winced.

Abel and a fumbling Sampson presented Wolberg with cards declaring that two trees would be planted in Israel to honor the memory of Harrison Wolberg. They were thanked and led into the living room where they were quietly introduced. About a dozen people were present, and enough food to satisfy several thousand Israeli troops.

Sampson cautiously surveyed the room. A full-length mirror was draped with black cloth, and the members of the immediate family sat on low stools. He nodded a greeting to Murray Wolberg, and stood next to Abel on the edge of the family circle. As T.J. had predicted, each member of the circle talked about the deceased, remembering his fine points, his virtues. Since the conversational ball was passed in an arbitrary sequence, Sampson found it hard to follow. He only snatched at it. Phrases came from round, white-haired Mrs. Wolberg, Harrison's mother: ". . . such a good boy;" ". . . always came home on weekends, except when the firm's business . . . ;" ". . . *shul* every Friday night . . . ;" ". . . didn't run around;" ". . . a devoted son." Others; outside of the family circle, added their remembrances: ". . . very active in the men's . . . ;" ". . . always could be counted on for help."

"Where's the john?" Sampson signed to Abel. The doctor nodded toward a hallway leading to the rear of the house. Again Sampson was caught off base. The bathroom mirror which ran the entire length of one wall was covered in black, a blackness which the soft, recessed overhead lights could not combat.

Zipping his fly, Sampson learned of his second gaffe. "Sorry," the girl said, taking a long look. "I did knock, you know." Fortunately, she stood directly under one of the dim lights so that he was able to make out what she said. A blessing, he supposed, as he stared at the door through which she finally left.

Good God! Deaf for three decades and he'd forgotten lesson number 1: always lock the bathroom door behind you. Well, actually, it was probably lesson number 50—at best. The absurdity of the situation, and the absurdities that might have been, made him laugh silently to himself.

"Really, I did knock," she repeated as Sampson nearly ran into her in the hallway. "Funny, wasn't it?"

"I'm deaf," he announced, and watched consternation flit across her face. But not for long.

"I'm Rachel. A cousin, twice removed, but everyone calls me Cousin Rachel. Did you read that book? I liked the movie better."

She was young, and taller than Sampson by a good three inches, even in her stocking feet. She had long black hair, large dark brown eyes, high cheekbones. Her wide mouth was just slightly streaked with red. Sampson found the trace of her sultry perfume appealing.

"Trehune," Sampson said, trying to speak softly.

"What?"

"Trehune."

She nodded, though he was sure she hadn't understood him. "Did you know Harrison well?"

"No."

"We were engaged. Well, not really—just that our families thought it was a good idea. But he was such a drag, and I knew he didn't really care for me. We just let our families keep talking about it. Nothing serious."

Sampson nodded. She continued to stand beside him, which made Sampson uncomfortable.

"You aren't Jewish, are you?" she asked.

"Not. I'm not."

"I'm not, either. Not really. I mean—all that." She nodded toward the living room. "My mother gets very upset with me."

Ironically, given her disclaimer, she brought back some long-forgotten words to Sampson. "Daughters of Jerusalem . . . thy stature is like to a palm tree and thy breasts to clusters of grapes, the joints of thy thighs are like jewels, the roof of thy mouth like the best wine." Sampson stepped back from her perfume. Hadn't he done enough for one night?

She didn't seem to notice, just talked on. "Are you married?"

He shook his head.

"I almost was, once. Not to Harrison, of course. A student at N.Y.U. I really dug him, if you know what I mean. But Mother wouldn't have it—him, I mean. I had to have an abortion. It was up at Altman's place, where Harrison died."

Sampson's mouth drooped slightly; he felt it.

"Don't look so old-fashioned. Nothing wrong with it. That clinic has a whole wing that looks more like a sorority house than part of a hospital. Lots of girls, from good families. You'd be surprised. They call it a D and C. That's dilatation and curettage. · You're only out for a few minutes, and they scrape—" Abruptly, she stopped and turned toward the living room. Sampson saw Seymour walk quickly toward the foyer. Apparently, the doorbell had rung.

Deo gratias, he thought. "Let's go," he signed to Abel when he rejoined him. Abel nodded and indicated they would leave in a few minutes.

Seymour Wolberg returned, accompanied by Dr. Altman, Morton Bannon, and a striking woman who was introduced as Constance Ellis Bannon. She was the daughter of that aging but powerful Senator from the South, Charles Ellis. She looked every inch the Southern aristocrat. She would probably continue looking that way until she was sixty.

She must be near fifty now, thought Sampson. But she could pass for thirty. Her well-controlled fullish figure smacked of Melba toast and cottage cheese. Finishing school or a bit of modeling had insured that her posture was effortlessly straight. She entered the room not dramatically, but gracefully, with smartness.

Her right hand, when Sampson took it, was slightly cool, with firm, satiny flesh. A rock of a diamond glittered on her left hand, in which she held a soft-leather purse. She must have heard of his deafness, since she kept her face turned toward him while she offered the usual polite phrases. Her eyes were empty, except for a trace of socially demanded warmth.

Probably a bedroom iceberg, thought Sampson, still captivated by the perfume of the sensuous Rachel. Wouldn't want her hair mussed, her skin cream disturbed, her necessary rest curtailed. Bannon did not stand close to her, but seemed to view her as he would a valuable sculpture he had acquired not for art's sake but for pride of ownership.

Although he was anxious to leave, Sampson made no objection when Abel indicated they should stay for a few more minutes. Sampson watched as Bannon, with calm assurance, talked about the late Harrison Wolberg. He mentioned that they had been friends since they roomed together in college and that he had the highest respect for Harry. He recounted an undergraduate incident, most of which Sampson couldn't see, but it had to do with Wolberg's sincerity. "He was the most honest man I have ever known," Bannon concluded. Sad, slight smiles and nods all around.

Mrs. Wolberg started again, citing more examples of Harrison's absolute integrity, even when it meant embarrassment or losing a client.

Altman remembered Wolberg as a friend and as a patient —a good, decent person. He offered his deepest regrets.

Her nerves finally giving way, Mrs. Wolberg began to sway from side to side on the verge of collapse. Her two remaining sons, Murray and Seymour, left their wives to help their mother down the hall into a bedroom. As she passed, she said clearly, "If only he hadn't gone up there. If only he hadn't gone there."

Seymour returned almost immediately and apologized to Dr. Altman, who seemed embarrassed. His mother was simply, naturally upset. No one blamed the doctor for what had happened to Harrison.

Sampson prodded Abel with an elbow and signed, "Now?" Abel nodded and they moved toward the door, where Seymour embraced each of them. "Thank you for your sympathy and friendship," he said to Sampson before he closed the door.

Sampson was necessarily quiet for most of the drive back

89

to the city, but when they merged with midtown traffic, he began badgering Abel to stop for a nightcap, until the doctor finally agreed. They chose Barney's, a tranquil neighborhood bar, two blocks from Sampson's apartment. Besides the bartender, there were only two customers, men who sat at the bar mesmerized by tapes of a football game played the previous weekend.

They settled into a rear booth, and when they had been served, Sampson signed Rachel's story.

"I'm sure Dr. Altman and his clinic are operating within the law," Abel replied pompously. "After all, just because a foolish girl lets drop a remark or two . . . These things are closely supervised by county medical boards. An undue number of D and C's would certainly bring down the wrath of the law."

"But suppose there was something going on at the Altman Clinic and Wolberg tumbled to it?"

"Need I remind you that the autopsy performed by three respected physicians revealed no foul play?" Abel continued in defense of the brotherhood. "Wolberg's heart simply stopped beating. No needle wounds, no poison, he simply—"

Sampson abruptly changed the subject. "What about Wolberg?" he signed. "What was his problem?"

"I certainly won't discuss any patient's case in detail, even if he's dead. Just take it from me that his complaint wasn't unique. Not uncommon for men of his age and position."

"He wasn't really a loony?"

"I do wish you wouldn't use that word. You know it's really a symptom of your own inadequacy. A few days ago, I was reading an article in the *Journal of Neuropsychiatric Medicine*. The author's hypothesis about handicapped persons—"

Sampson closed his eyes, drummed his fingers on the table,

and counted to thirty slowly. When he opened his eyes, Abel had stopped speaking and was staring at him.

"Well, since you don't want to listen . . ." Abel reached for his wallet.

"Wolberg. What was his handicap? Could it have anything to do with his death?"

"Hardly," Abel spelled. Since his mouth hung open for a moment, he must have sighed. "Harrison Wolberg—and I stress that this is confidential, that I'm telling you this so you will stop scratching around for something that isn't there— Harrison Wolberg suffered from mild impotency."

"*Mild* impotency?" Sampson underlined the word in the air.

"*Quiet.* The point is, I can't see where it would have made him dangerous or a threat to anyone."

"Could the right kind of woman cure the condition?"

"Such cures have been reported but, of course, no permanent cure can be effected until its deep-seated psychological causes are alleviated."

"Could he have led a double life?"

"You jest. Harrison was the most conservative, unimaginative sort of person. I suppose you would call him colorless."

"Brown. Come back to Hastings with me tomorrow."

Abel looked at Sampson as if he had suddenly, finally gone mad.

"I want to see Voisin again. I want to hear again."

"I can understand that. But under the circumstances it's not likely that Voisin will be treating anyone in Hastings. Given the publicity, he probably won't want to treat anyone in the United States."

"Tomorrow."

Abel was exasperated. "You are just being bullheaded. As

a matter of fact, I think we were lucky to get out of that town with so little trouble. I'd be perfectly happy never to set foot in Hastings again."

"Yes, but suppose . . ."

"I have my patients to consider. I can't just take off and leave them. They depend on me; we have a very close relationship."

"So do we. This acupuncture thing was your idea." This was a lie, but Sampson had learned a long time ago that an appeal to conscience garnished with a suggestion of guilt usually worked on Abel. "I *have* to see Voisin again." He kept after Abel until the doctor reluctantly agreed to think about it.

"But not tomorrow, definitely not. Friday, maybe. I could meet you up there."

"I'm leaving in the morning," said Sampson.

This time Abel took out his wallet and paid the bill. The two parted at the corner, Abel going back to his car for a short drive home, Sampson to his apartment and a walk with Savvy.

That done, he puttered around restlessly, chucking out accumulated advertisements, washing the morning's few dishes, all the while arranging and rearranging a variety of "ifs," "buts," and "supposes." Finally he poured himself a giant-size Scotch, plugged in the fan, and took off his shoes and socks. Then he turned on his phonograph and pulled a comfortable chair directly in front of it. Neighbors be damned, he thought, reaching for a record. The moment he saw what the Boss was up to, Savvy took off as if pursued by all hell's furies. Safety was at the other end of the apartment, underneath Sampson's bed.

At least an hour had passed when Sampson felt the fan's breeze across his bare feet. Someone was at the door.

"Hi," said Sadie, the widowed earth mother with matrimony forever on her mind. Sampson was cast as the groom.

He read her greeting, waved her in, went to turn the phonograph off. She probably hadn't even heard herself speak.

"Knew you were in," she said unnecessarily. Undoubtedly there were times when she regretted helping Sampson get his record player. A couple of years before, Sampson had confided his belief that, under optimum conditions, he would probably be able to hear the lower end of the musical scale.

"Let's find out," she had said, and promptly called her brother-in-law. A friend of his had put together a sound system to Sampson's specifications. Its key component was an ancient but topnotch Altec-Lansing speaker, 24 inches, cone type, with a high-cut, low-pass frequency filter; it was fed by a 200-watt amplifier.

That first night, Sampson had played the only three records he had, over and over again. He had sat hunched in front of the speaker which was placed in a wall so that the entire adjacent room, his study, acted as a sounding board. He began tapping his fingers in time to what he heard. It was almost dawn before he went to bed.

"How was it?" asked Sadie the next afternoon, a Sunday.

"Wonderful," said Sampson. "I'll show you."

Two minutes later, Sadie had walked over to the phonograph, then to the amplifier, and finally to the speaker. She pointed to a small dangling porcelain insulator. "Sampson," she said sadly, "you can't hear anything. The connection to the speaker isn't working. You probably had the volume up too high last night, maybe blew it out. Or maybe you blew a tube. I don't know. When you want, Al can come back and fix it." Then she had left, without another word.

Sampson spent that Sunday alone, getting plastered, cursing

God, but mostly berating himself. He'd been taken in again, allowed himself to hope. Like an idiot, he had chalked up a success where there was none. He hated that contraption.

But it was there. Six months later, he said to Sadie, "I'm going to try again." Just in time for Christmas, the set was repaired and the volume dial notched to indicate the upper limits which the system could tolerate. This time, Sampson took off his socks and shoes, a common practice among the deaf; his bare feet, placed flat on the floor near the speaker, helped him pick up sound vibrations. This time, he stacked four Bach organ disks on the spindle.

By New Year's Eve, he was sure he could identify the tempo and timbre of each record. He called in T.J. and Sadie for a test. Without Sampson's seeing the jacket or label, one of them would place a record on the turntable. He missed the first one but scored on all the rest.

"Bach, Prelude and Fugue in C Minor," he said about the second record. When he was sure his friends weren't deceiving him, he broke into a rare wide grin. The happiest New Year's Eve ever.

"Tired?" Sampson asked Sadie now. As always, she was fashionably dressed, but her graying ringlets drooped into her eyes and her make-up had worn away.

"You bet. I just wanted to say hello. Arnold told me about Sunday night. I'm sorry." Arnold was T.J., whom Sadie usually addressed as Mr. Heppish. "I would have stopped by sooner but I was very busy."

Sampson nodded. The amount of energy and brain draining required by Sadie's work frequently amazed him. She was the advertising director of a New York department store.

"We've been working late every night since Monday. We're mounting a new campaign to push a shipment of men's underwear. The newspaper ad has to have high product visibility and consumer appeal, but must be in good taste. That's difficult."

Sampson nodded again. He couldn't imagine anything less appealing than a picture of men's underwear.

"Hungry? Like an omelet?" he asked. Usually the shoe was on the other foot. Sadie plied him with the likes of stuffed grape leaves, which she claimed to adore. Sampson didn't believe her.

"O.K.," she said. A wonderful thing about Sadie: she never talked too much.

Sampson padded after her toward the kitchen where they were joined by Savvy, who, as usual, gave the woman now curled up in one of the large captain's chairs a haughty sniff. It was the least he could do. The woman had cats. A pair of uppity Siamese.

There was a companionable silence while Sampson fixed the omelet and put on some water for Sadie's tea. "What are you going to do now?" she asked when Sampson sat down.

"Don't really know," he said.

Revived by the snack, Sampson decided to tell Sadie about his evening at the Wolbergs', the young woman in the picture, his visit to the Ticker Tap, and his trip to Chinatown. But he really wasn't up to talking any more; nor did he want the strain of concentrating on a Hearer's face and gestures. He'd had more than enough of that already today.

Without saying anything, he went to his study and returned with two felt-tipped pens and two lined, yellow legal pads. Hitching his chair closer to Sadie's, he began: "Wolbergs' tonight. *Shivah*. Met girl. Curious tale."

"Bizarre! Shouldn't get involved" were the last words Sadie scrawled across her pad an hour later. At the doorway, she said, "How about dinner tomorrow night? My place. The copy has to be at the newspapers by noon tomorrow. I'm taking the rest of the day and Friday off."

"Can't," said Sampson. "Going to Hastings. Got to see Voisin. Got to find out."

She didn't ask what, just smiled and shook her head. A good thing, he thought, unplugging the fan, because he really didn't know.

EIGHT

Sampson wished he were standing on the Mount in Hastings, England, next to the ruins of Britain's first Norman castle. He wished he were in Hastings, New Zealand, a place he had at least heard of. Or even running sand through his fingers on that solitary speck in the Papuan Islands labeled Hastings. Anywhere but in Hastings, Connecticut, playing the fool again. He sipped his Scotch, not because he was especially thirsty but simply to kill time. Apparently, he was going to have a lot of it to do away with. For the past three hours, he had attempted to find Henri Voisin. No one at the Blue Coat had seen him. If he ate, he took his meals elsewhere, for neither the waitresses nor the room-service bellhop recalled serving him.

Ye Olde Colonial Restaurante was L-shaped, with the short leg forming a cocktail lounge, away from the bustle of the open dining room. Sampson was slumped in a booth, moodily looking around, finding things to be irritated by. Amid the fake leather and fake brass furnishings, a facsimile hurricane lamp flickered, and a Quainte Ashtraye squatted on the formica-top table. He surveyed the long wall of the lounge. Its laminated panels held plastic harpoons, plastic sailing vessels in bottles, and plastic flotsam from an unseen shipwreck. A length of artificial ship's rope scalloped beneath the clutter. Fortunately, the bar itself was well stocked and guarded by a surprisingly competent bartender who read the racing form during every spare moment.

As Sampson unconsciously stirred ice with his finger, he saw a shadow cover part of the table, and looked up to the smiling face of Abel. He squelched his delight in his friend's appearance, remembering that he was grumpy. "What happened to your loonies?" he signed curtly.

The doctor slid into the booth and faced Sampson. "One failed to keep his appointment at ten, and another called to cancel her three-o'clock session, which left only—"

Sampson cut him off. "Obviously they're getting better. Checked in yet?"

Abel nodded, showing Sampson the room number on his key. "I'm on the other side," Sampson commented with compact gestures. "I got Wolberg's room, 204, second floor. The boy wonder at the desk told me that Wolberg was here for over a week. Doing what, I wonder."

Abel shrugged and tried to get the bartender's attention.

"Self-service. No waitresses till six."

Abel got up and moved to the bar. When he returned with his drink, the bartender followed him, placing another Scotch in front of Sampson.

"What makes you special?" Abel wanted to know.

"Alas."

"What?"

Wearily, Sampson repeated, this time moving his left hand closer to the doctor's face and spelling the word. Hand in a fist, thumb straight along the side: *A*. Hand in a fist, thumb extended, forefinger raised straight up: *L*. Fist, thumb straight: *A*. Fist, thumb tucked beneath the clenched fingers: *S*.

Abel waited.

"Alas. Out of Duke Fleet by Marvelous Jones. Scratched today, but probably be in ninth tomorrow. Long odds. Sure thing." Abel knew that Sampson's hunches were frequently profitable, and Sampson knew that Abel Strongly Disapproved of gambling on moral and psychological grounds. Each man was about to launch into his favorite speech on the subject when Abel's expression changed and Sampson knew someone was approaching behind him. Before he could turn his head, he felt a hard shove on the shoulder and he was shunted farther into the booth by Claire Fletcher. Her arrival had been accomplished with all the subtlety of a brick dropped into a mud puddle.

Sampson looked at her closely, struck by the difference between the woman he had last seen and the one who now mouthed greetings. Her hair was a trifle straggly, obviously not getting its accustomed care. She wore an attractive black-and-green cocktail dress, rushing the hour, since it was only 4:30. Again she looked out of place.

As she spoke, he watched her face, which was fatigued and only partially made up. Little pouches had appeared beneath her green eyes, which shone too brightly; she had the look of a cat about to pounce.

She waved at the bartender and was ignored as the man busied himself with a couple of lawyerish arrivals now holding down the two end stools. He mixed their drinks, ignored her signals from the booth, and returned to the racing form.

"Shitty service," Fletcher declared, probably loud enough for the whole lounge to hear. Embarrassed but always the gentleman, Abel offered to do the honors. "Thanks, dear," she said. "A martini, double, straight-up, dry, with a twist." While Abel stood at the bar overseeing her order, she turned to Sampson. "You two here for the circus tomorrow?" It took him a second to realize that she was referring to Henri Voisin's hearing for contempt of court. "Promises to be in-

98

teresting, doesn't it? I might have something to add when the time comes."

She continued, neither desiring nor needing any response from Sampson. Many Hearers were like that. "I've got a feeling. I've had to rewrite this little piece I was doing on acupuncture—let's see—three times now. And each time it gets longer and more involved. In my racket, that usually only happens when some clown in the federal government screws up, and with each denial more of the truth leaks out. You know, like the Watergate mess."

Abel set her drink in front of her and for a moment she was strangely quiet, studying the lamp's wavering flame. "Cheers, dears," she said, and swallowed thirstily.

"Where's Eggers?" Sampson probed. That was practically his last chance, and she didn't even answer the question. From then on, she alternately flattered and badgered the two men, frequently with disconcerting directness. "What did you find out at Wolberg Brothers?" she asked Sampson. "Did that old fool know anything?" Abel frowned, unaware of Sampson's trip to the brokerage firm, and Sampson simply shook his head. Still she persisted, stalking, circling, lunging in for the quick thrust. "You mean you've been here since early afternoon and you haven't spoken to Voisin at all?" she demanded.

"No. Have you?"

"Of course not, or I wouldn't be asking you. What about you, Doctor?"

Abel replied that he had not seen Dr. Voisin since Monday morning when he'd been taken away by two policemen.

"He was released that same afternoon," Fletcher said, "but they picked up his passport to make sure he would be around for his contempt hearing tomorrow. He checked into the Blue Coat that same day and he's been here ever since. But I arrived this morning, and haven't seen a sign of him. Telephoned him every hour, left messages which he hasn't picked up. Desk clerk says he hasn't seen him." This much Sampson knew was true, for he had also tried to reach Voisin on the house telephone. His message had been filed by the desk clerk, who had not seen Voisin since he came on duty at 8 A.M.

"Cashier says he hasn't been in for any meals, either," Fletcher continued, ticking off points on the fingers of her right hand. "The old geezer at the train station swore he hadn't sold him a ticket. Knew who he was right off, and how he was supposed to stay in Hastings until Friday. That silly fool of a cabdriver hasn't seen him, either. Are you sure . . . ?" Sampson had to admire her tenacity. She wouldn't win any popularity prizes, but she was a thoroughgoing, professional reporter. I would hate to have her on my back, thought Sampson.

Abel broke off in midsentence and stood up. Fletcher twisted in the booth and pressed quite close to Sampson, her bare arm resting on the back of the booth. He had a brief impression of an odor. She's perspiring, he thought; she must be nervous. If anything, the lounge seemed on the cool side.

He got up as far as the table allowed and accepted the patrician hand of Constance Bannon. Her husband reached over and squeezed firmly. Dr. Richard Altman, who was with them, was unable to get frontage on the small table and just waved in a mock salute.

"But you've got to eat," Morton Bannon was saying to Abel, "so come on and join us. We'll get that big old table in the corner and have a real feast. On me. I insist." He eased Abel out from behind the table by the arm and next turned his attention to Fletcher, who offered little opposition. Sampson was included in the invitation, and he accepted because he didn't want to seem a boor and because someone might let drop a tidbit of news. Or get it yanked out by Fletcher. Nevertheless, he had a feeling about the kind of dinner it was going to be. He was right.

100

Reluctantly separating himself from the racing form, the bartender dimmed the lights. Constance Bannon, seated on Sampson's left, began easily enough, always turning to face him when she spoke. With Abel's help, Sampson was at least aware of the topic under discussion. He ordered a steak, rare, and told himself it wouldn't be too bad. Slowly, despite the efforts of Abel, he was cut out of the conversation. To include him, especially after a second round of drinks, was just too much trouble.

Over the third round, Sampson watched Altman play straight man for Bannon, who had flung himself into the role of entertainer with frenetic energy. Buoyancy or nerves? Evidently Bannon was not always so ebullient, because his wife looked at him with faint but happy surprise.

"Would you pass me the cheese dip?" she asked Sampson. Half rising to reach the crock of tasteless whipped cheese, he was suddenly aware that she was laughing uproariously. My God, was his fly open? No. It seemed Bannon had just told a real corker.

"*Cheese*, Mrs. Bannon," Sampson fairly snarled as he smacked it down in front of her, but she was busy showing her teeth and barely noticed. Rebuffed, he curled himself up on his ice floe and watched them float away on theirs. It had happened hundreds of times. Still. Damn Hearers. He closed his eyes and searched for an appropriate quotation from The Book. Finally, he settled on one: "I might have known," said Eeyore. "After all, one can't complain. I have my friends. Sombody spoke to me only yesterday. And was it last week or the week before that Rabbit bumped into me and said 'Bother!' The Social Round. Always something going on."

The service was slow. The rare steak he had ordered arrived medium-well. Nurse Harmon wandered in, looking cool and assured in a revealing blue silk blouse. Although no one had extended an invitation, she joined them, pulling up a chair between Altman and Fletcher. As a result, Sampson could barely move his arms to cut his steak. The dessert, Ye Olde Original Browne Bettye, was suitably wretched. But finally it was over.

Although it was only nine, Sampson felt exhausted and distinctly antisocial—or, more accurately, anti-Hearer. He was not at all enthusiastic, therefore, when Bannon suggested they adjourn for a party at his house. "Just a five-minute drive, and a well-stocked bar. We can sample some of the punch I'll be serving at Saturday's celebration of Bannon's new issue."

Sampson was surprised to see that Claire Fletcher had also declined—much to Bannon's disappointment, apparently. Odd. The few decipherable snatches of conversation at dinner had been from Fletcher. He understood them because she pursued the same questions as she had earlier, with renewed vigor. Abel, however, had accepted. Over coffee he had discovered that both Altman and Bannon played chess. With regular devotion, according to Mrs. Bannon. He'll be oblivious for hours, thought Sampson.

As he climbed the stairs to his room, Sampson was reminded of his first meeting with Belinda Shaw. He would like to see Shaw tonight. Any night, for that matter. But he had rejected the idea of a meeting with her. He had made a bit of a fool of himself with her once, and he was not about to do it again.

He paused, key at the ready, and decided to try to find Henri Voisin one more time. His room was across the hall, down one door, and Sampson pounded vigorously. To hell with politeness, he thought. Voisin might be on the other side hollering "Go away" at him, or perhaps "Come in." He had no way of knowing, but the matter troubling his mind was much too important to be pushed aside. He pounded again. And again. No luck.

As he turned, he walked squarely into Claire Fletcher, and felt her bones against him. "Any luck?" she asked, and banged briefly on the door herself. "Let's you and me have a talk, Mr. Trehune, shall we?" she suggested at last. "Can I call you Sampson?" She walked to the room directly opposite Sampson's and was about to open the door, but stopped. "Let's have a nightcap. Come on, I'll buy. I don't do that very often, so you should take advantage of me while you've got the chance." She smiled in a parody of coyness.

In the lounge again, Sampson, savoring his Benedictine, gazed in awe as Fletcher began another martini, her fifth as far as he could remember, and all doubles. Not that she showed her drinks. She was loquacious and fidgety, but not from the gin.

"Why are you so anxious to see Voisin?" she asked, getting down to business.

Sampson pulled his right ear, indicating his deafness.

She curled her lip impatiently. "You expect me to believe that's the only reason? Come on, give. We might be able to help each other." Sampson at first doubted that, but then decided she might be right, after all.

"Why are you?" he finally countered.

"Cagey, aren't you? Well, pretend I smell a story. I want to be the first to get it. Satisfied?"

He wasn't. She had earlier made a remark about the next day's contempt hearing, and how she might have something to add. If there is a story, Sampson thought, she's got it already and is just fishing.

"Voisin is very interesting," Sampson said. "Fascinating."

"One could say that, couldn't one?" She smiled to herself, enjoying some private joke. Sampson studied her for a moment, and reviewed quickly everything he had learned over the past three days. Deciding to play a hunch, he added, "Whoever he is."

Her response was immediate, with no attempt at dissembling. She had heard and understood at once. "Well, well, well. You are full of surprises, Mr. Trehune." She gazed at him with honest admiration. "Shall we share, sort of pool our resources until we can confront that needle-happy nut? Then it's every man for himself, O.K.?"

Sampson nodded.

"Who is he?" she asked suddenly, with such intensity that Sampson was sure she herself didn't know.

"Don't know yet," he answered carefully, deciding to let himself be guided by her responses. "Do you?"

"No. But I'll find out." He waited, and she finally began talking openly. "It was Muntz—he put me on the track. Thought he knew Voisin from somewhere, so I decided to find out. Dr. Muntz was mistaken about knowing him, but the questions I asked opened up a real can of worms." She drained her martini. "You heard Voisin Monday? All right, not heard. But do you know he supposedly holds a degree from the University of Ulm? I got to thinking, why would a Frenchie go to a German school? And when Muntz chimed in about knowing him, I got really interested. I called in a few favors. A stringer for a mag I'm syndicated to lives near Ulm, in Blaubeuren. Turned him loose and guess what he found."

Sampson used her dramatic pause to take a swallow. The syrupy warmth delighted him, but he kept his eyes on Fletcher.

She leaned conspiratorially across the table. "The only Henri Voisin ever to graduate from the University of Ulm was a physician, and the university records indicate the date of graduation checks with Voisin's statement. But Henri Voisin was killed almost twenty years ago."

Sampson tried to keep the shock of surprise from showing in his face. He nodded. "And?"

"What d'you mean—and? The guy's a fake! That's enough to start with, isn't it? And when I get back to New York, I'll really go to work on him. Now, what have you got?"

He was saved from answering by the arrival of Belinda

Shaw, who paused by their table. "Miss Fletcher, Mr. Trehune. I heard you were back. Both of you," she added somewhat pointedly. "I hope—"

Fletcher cut in on her. "It's a nice town, Miss Prosecutor. Was there something you wanted?"

"No. Should there be?" she asked, all sweetness. "I just happened to stop by to speak with Dr. Voisin. I know that's a bit irregular, but there are so many things in this case which are irregular. When I saw you two together . . ."

Now it was Sampson's turn to interrupt. "Leaving," he said, and smiled.

Fletcher's glare held menace. "We'll have to talk again, Mr. Trehune," she said. "Soon."

NINE

Eyes tightly shut as if squinting for a better look at the filmstrip playing in his head, the black-haired man chuckled, rolled over onto his left side, and swatted his pillow in private delight. The bedside clock swept an hour away. The reels changed. The hands became fists and the knees drew up toward the chin.

He was there again. Eight years old and trapped in that ugly-smelling hospital, trapped in a gigantic bed with snow-cold sheets. They had done something mean to him. Far away, at the foot of the bed, stood his mother and father, familiar yet pulled out of shape. He watched them move their lips—and hoped. But nothing came out. Once more the evil parade began. White-sheathed witch doctors stuck things into his ears, making sure of their wicked work. Deliberately, he threw his dinner dishes on the floor, and saw them smash. Saw—but heard nothing. No reassuring sound followed the splintering plates as they slid across the floor.

He *knew* that there was nothing wrong with him. He felt fine. So it must be the hospital. They were making some monstrous experiment on him. If only he could get out of the hospital, he knew he would hear again, just like before.

He slid cautiously from the bed, weaved toward the door, opened it, and peered out. Two adults passed him, smiling and moving their lips. But they must have been part of the experiment, for he heard nothing. At least, they did not notice him. Turning a corner, hugging the walls, trying to keep out of sight, he searched for a way out.

Opening a door, he saw a little blond-haired girl, about his own age. She waved and moved her lips, but nothing came out. Even other kids, he thought bitterly.

Once more he crept around a corner. Suddenly and painfully, he was knocked down by a strange bed with huge wheels. A pretty-smelling nurse bent over him, quickly moving her lips and looking frightened. A white-coat came. More empty lip motion, the nurse pointing and gesturing. Finally, white-coat plucked him up and carried him back to his trap, that wretched bed.

Legs kicked sheet and lightweight blanket away and a hand reached up to tug at the top pajama button, which pulled against his throat. Still the man slept. Gradually his panting slowed to measured, deep breaths while he waited for the operator to splice the broken film. With tiny jerks, the second hand made fifteen rounds before the body twitched defensively against a fall.

106

Trapped in another strange bed. What held him now was intangible, but real. Fingers trembling, he tried to push against walls that were not there. Wherever he was, he knew he had to get out. He seemed surrounded by a fog that never lifted, and he had the terrifying premonition that this fog was all he would ever know again. He was certain he would die in this fog.

But he wasn't gone yet. He could feel the sweat under his arms, down his back; he could feel his heart heaving against his chest, his lungs, ready to burst, gasping for oxygen that was not there. He could taste fear rising in his throat. With a somehow pleasing, warm sensation of pain and terror, he tried to sit up in this strange bed. He had to make an effort. Not an effort to escape, for he had learned long ago that escape was impossible. But an effort to protest, to let them know that he existed and soon would no longer exist, and that they could not so simply, so casually, do this to him! He would scream a mighty scream, an epic scream. He gathered himself. Then, through the annihilating gray which vaporized all within its reach, he saw a wall.

The scream died within him. There was still hope. If walls existed, then other things outside this damnable gray fog existed, too. He would find out. But he had to find out soon, for he was choking, could hardly breathe.

At this moment, Sampson Trehune recognized that he was fully awake. He had not heard the crackling of the flames as they ate their way down the corridor toward his room; he had not heard the shouts, the screams, or the siren of the lone Hastings fire truck as it howled through the night toward the blaze. But he knew now he was awake—and damned near dead.

Quickly he sorted past from present. He was in bed in a room in the Blue Coat Hotel, and that room was burning up around him. That much was real, for, just as in the final minutes of his dreaming, he could hardly breathe. The smoke rapidly filling the room tasted oily, and made him gag. He moved toward the door, but tripped and fell against the wall. The wall felt warm, almost hot. "Damn," he roared, and choked. He had better keep his mouth shut.

Feeling along the wall, trying to reach the door, he banged his ankle on a low table in a corner, cursed, and choked. Reversing his gropings, his hand soon touched the molding which outlined the doorframe. Then he had the door; then he grabbed the doorknob, gasped in pain, inhaled a mouthful of smoke, and choked again. The metal doorknob was searing hot.

Mechanically, he pulled out his pajama shirt, wrapped it around his hand, and reached toward the doorknob again. He caught himself just in time, thinking, the doorknob is hot because there is intense heat right outside the door. How intense? Too damn hot for me to walk through.

Stumbling, he crossed the room to the window, eyes burning, tears cooling his face. The lower part of the window was completely blocked by an air conditioner, sealed tightly, escape impossible.

Choking, weeping, cursing, he was dead and he knew it.

But an instinct for propriety, ridiculous under the circumstances, saved him. The very air in the room seemed to burn his throat and, because of the oily smoke, he gagged. He was going to be sick; he fought against it, but could taste the vomit in his mouth. He clamped his jaws shut.

"Don't get sick on the rug," a voice from somewhere in his past chided. "Get to the bathroom. The bathroom is where people go to get sick." The bathroom.

He pushed the door open and stumbled in, closing it behind him. Though small, the room still had some air. For end-

108

less seconds, he bent over the toilet bowl and was sick, his stomach twisting from smoke and fear.

Turning, he opened the door briefly and smoke poured in, along with a wave of air that was so hot it ignited the loose strands of his hair. Flames crawled up the walls, filling the bedroom. He slammed the door and, slapping his head to put out the burning hair, became almost hysterical. He turned on the faucets and water poured out, for a few seconds. Then stopped.

Choking, he lunged for the toilet. Steadying himself on the rim of the shower enclosure, he removed the toilet-tank cover, and threw water on his face. Soaking a towel, he drew breath through its wet folds and found momentary relief. He touched the bathroom door for support, and felt his wet hand sizzle.

At that moment, he felt the vibrations of a crash shaking the hotel structure beneath his bare feet.

"No, no, no," he protested into the wet towel covering his face. He climbed onto the toilet bowl and reached over the sink toward the window—the small, narrow, painted-shut window that was his last chance for survival. He pushed and tugged. Nothing. He knelt on the washbasin and pushed again. Nothing. Weeping, choking with smoke, frustration, and rage, he beat against the window. The pane shattered.

Air. He could breathe a bit. The smoke was being drawn out. And the draft was bringing heat, and flames, from the other room. Wrapping the towel around his fist, he knocked out the remaining pieces of glass and stuffed himself into the small opening.

And got stuck. O God, O Mon Maison, O desserts of all varieties, never again. Never, I swear. Inanely, given the moment, he thought of Pooh and absurdly hoped Rabbit's friends and relations would *aid him in his sore distress.*

109

He wiggled, pulled, wrenched, ripped his pajamas and several inches of skin around his abdomen, tore himself free, and tumbled onto the narrow roof just a foot below the window.

He caught hold of the ledge, felt a rush of scalding air sweep through the broken window, and pushed himself away.

Edging farther away from the inferno which the window had become, he looked around and down toward the ground. Dizziness seized him, and he sank to his knees. Nausea shook him, and his hands clutched his stomach. The trees, the bushes, the flames licking the window frame he had just crawled through, the dark sky, the stars—all began to spin and finally merge into one mad, distorted picture. He was falling, returning to the gray fog, to his own personal trap.

TEN

It was only through sheer perversity that Sampson goaded himself into consciousness. The gods tried to convince him that he wanted to die, but he thought otherwise, despite the sure sensory knowledge that he was in a strange bed.

He rubbed his eyes and, without moving, looked around, automatically taking in his surroundings. Hospital, his brain shouted. Disinfectant and too-white sheets. The door to his left opened and a white-capped female appeared, and disappeared. As he glanced her way, Sampson saw the watch on the bedside table. He snatched it up with his left hand. Arm and shoulder muscles protested.

It was still running and showed 9:10. The sun was visible

through the slots of the blind. Morning, therefore. The calendar dial of the watch indicated it was Friday. Last night was Thursday, Thursday in Hastings. Probably in the Altman Clinic, he thought, pleased with his deductions so far. But why?

Then he remembered.

The fire; it was real. His mouth filled with the thick taste of smoke and he gagged. He thought about moving. Should he? Cut off from the distractions of a sound-filled world, Sampson had become more attuned to his body than most people were. He relaxed and read the messages it sent him. He moved slightly, flexing, tightening, extending. In a few moments, he knew there was nothing seriously wrong with him. Left leg felt stiff, both his shoulders ached, and when he moved his lips his face stung—probably scratched. But there was nothing serious, nothing that he could feel. That was good enough.

He sat up slowly and swung his legs off the bed. Everything inside him seemed to be functioning. Stiffly, he stood, and turned around. He poured a glass of stale, tepid water from a metal carafe and dumped it back in. He limped over to the basin in the corner of the room, filled the glass with cold tap water, rinsed his mouth, and spat. Better. He filled the glass again, and gulped it down. Then another. Suddenly he knew he was going to be violently, painfully sick.

That typified for Sampson the response which he had to the next three hours or so. At last, he looked up from the bowl, quivering, and found he was being helped by a pink-faced young boy in a white jacket. Supported, Sampson made it back to his bed.

His head resting gratefully on a thick down pillow, he breathed in slowly, deeply. A few moments, and he was sitting up again, feeling much better. The pink face of his rescuer was still there, looking worried. Sampson reached toward the

111

table, remembered the fire and that he had probably lost everything. "Cigarette?" he asked as politely as he could, repeating the request when the face looked puzzled. Finally, he was handed a pack, took one, lit it, and inhaled. Satisfactory, he thought, coughing.

He finished the cigarette, and looked at pink-face, wondering if he should ask for another. The man who stood respectfully at the foot of Sampson's bed raised his hand, a nervous gesture as if he were coughing or clearing his throat. What does he want, Sampson wondered.

"Mr. Trehune, I'm Dr.—"

Sampson's eyes dropped from the face and examined the jacket. There, sticking its ugly form out of the right pocket, was an obscene thing, a weapon of torture: a large, silver tuning fork. Now he knew what pink-face wanted. He could feel his mastoid bone already vibrating in anticipation.

He looked up as the man approached him. Patiently, Sampson allowed the prods and squeezes and twists and thumps which the doctor inflicted upon him. But when the hand reached for the chart and the questions began, Sampson had had enough.

"Nothing broken," the pink face said. "Guess you were lucky." Sampson said nothing, just glared. He did not want to be accused of lending encouragement. "About last night, Mr. Trehune. They couldn't get much of a story from you when you were in the emergency room."

"I fell from a narrow, second-story roof while trying not to be incinerated."

"Yes, I see. Fell, you say. Ever had fainting spells before? Or moments when you felt you were falling?"

Balefully, Sampson looked at him, and answered, as distinctly as he was able, "Ménière's disease: dizziness, nausea, vertigo. Common in deaf with damage to inner ear. Rarely bothers me, except when fleeing burning buildings."

112

Pink-face did not look pleased. "Yes, well, I guess you were lucky. I understand that your fall was broken by a row of hedges. New landscaping on that side of the hotel. I would say you were very lucky."

That did it. Sampson decided it was his turn to pontificate. He closed his eyes, relaxed, let his voice find the range where it was most comfortable. "Lucky. If I had been born in Athens, Aristotle would have labeled me mentally defective and dropped me in a river. Romans no better. Saint Augustine would damn me to hell because, he said, 'knowledge of God comes only through hearing.' According to *De Pontificale Romanum*—fourteenth century, only a dozen copies extant— I would be asked a question or two at time went deaf. Did not answer suitably, be excommunicated. Spend rest of life in dungeon being prayed over. Lucky! Why, in these enlightened times . . ." And he rambled on, letting the bitterness pour out of him, until finally he felt his voice crack and he knew that even the most attentive listener could not understand his words. But he felt much better. Refreshed. He opened his eyes and actually smiled.

The pink face was standing near the door and looking worried and silly. Abel was at the foot of the bed, lips pursed in concern. Dr. Altman was beside him, a hypodermic syringe in his hand. The smile vanished from Sampson's face.

"No!" he insisted, and pulled his arm away from the doctor's reaching hand.

Altman drew back, surprised, and looked pleadingly at Abel, who said, "For your own good. You were raving."

"Bullshit!"

Surprised, the three doctors exchanged glances.

"He'll be all right," Abel finally said, adjusting his face to its long-suffering, martyred expression. He nodded, and both Altman and pink-face left the room.

113

Alone, the two just looked at each other for a moment, each glad that the other was alive.

"If I'm all right, how come I'm stuck in here?" Sampson's fingers asked.

"Just a precaution. To make sure there are no internal injuries. No concussions which escaped detection. Sometimes the symptoms don't appear for hours, even days after an injury. Relax, enjoy yourself."

"B-u-l-l-s-h-i-t," Sampson spelled.

"It could be worse, you know."

Sampson scowled. Here comes the "How Lucky You Are So Just Shut Up" speech again, he thought.

"Claire Fletcher's dead."

Yes, it could be worse. "Anyone else?"

"No, just her."

Sampson was truly shocked. For several minutes, he lay there blinking at the sunlight as it filtered through the blinds. He was just beginning to like Fletcher. She had character, he had decided the previous night. She had daring, style. She was not just a colorless blob. Now she was . . . The memory of a charred body he had once seen swept over him. He would have been sick, but there was nothing left inside him. "Burned?" he asked.

"Suffocated."

"Smoke?"

Abel shook his head. "Probably a pillow over her head. Can't really be sure. I was with Altman at the autopsy. Fire only singed her hair, burned her shoes off, second- and third-degree burns on lower extremities. But the cause of death definitely was suffocation. Before the fire, since there was no smoke in her lungs."

At that moment, Lieutenant Hodges peeked in the door, looking timid—which Sampson knew was not his natural state. "Come in," Sampson said.

114

Hodges apologized for disturbing him, emphasizing that he knew just how Mr. Trehune must feel. However, if he could just spare a few moments, and so forth. God, how tedious officialdom can be, Sampson thought.

The officer looked at Abel, who turned and was about to leave. Quickly Sampson signed, "You stay or I say nothing. Can't talk," he signed, lying.

Abel translated the signs for Hodges, who agreed, reluctantly, to the doctor's presence. Like most people, the lieutenant was uncomfortable when others communicated without his understanding. He put on the face of authority and began: "What can you tell me about last night? Just what happened, as you recall?"

"I don't know. I was asleep," Sampson signed, and Abel spoke the words to Hodges, who nodded and jumped right back in. "Yes, but did you see or hear anything unusual— Sorry, scratch that last. But did you notice anything, anything at all?"

Mollified, Sampson thought hard, and signed to Abel, "Smoke. I swallowed whole mouthfuls of smoke. Greasy, oily smoke."

When Abel relayed this to Hodges, the lieutenant was still for a moment, then asked, "Are you quite positive?"

"Of course!" Sampson signed furiously. "Greasy smoke— I can still taste it." He made a motion, as if indicating he was going to be sick.

Hodges jotted a few lines in the leather notebook he was holding. "You were in Room 204—is that correct, Mr. Trehune?"

Sampson assented.

"And you noticed nothing suspicious?"

"N-O," spelled in large movements, using both hands.

"The desk clerk tells me you left a message for Dr. Voisin. Several messages. In fact, he said that you tried to reach him continually, most of yesterday afternoon and evening. Even before you went up to your room when you arrived, you had the clerk ring Voisin's room, and also had him paged in the restaurant. Did you ever catch up with Voisin, Mr. Trehune?" Hodges looked up, all innocence, pencil poised.

What's going on? Sampson wondered. "No." He spoke for the first.time, startling Hodges.

"Not at all? Not even a word or two? Never saw him, in or out of the hotel?"

"No," Sampson said again. He signed to Abel, "What in hell is all this?" His friend questioned the lieutenant.

"Well, I suppose there's no harm in telling you. This sort of thing gets around fast. First, your account of the fire squares with something our initial investigation discovered, something supported by the testimony of the six firemen who were the first on the scene, as well as several other guests and hotel employees. The fire began in your wing of the hotel, Mr. Trehune. On your floor. And it wasn't accidental; it was arson. The way we figure it, a person or persons unknown removed several of the hurricane lamps from the restaurant, or perhaps merely tapped the drum of kerosene kept in the kitchen to fill them. Doesn't matter much which. Next, a trail of kerosene was splashed down the hallway, soaking the carpet and the lower walls. Then the fire door at the end of the hall was propped open and 'Pooooff!'" Hodges threw up his hands quickly.

Sampson absorbed this, said nothing.

"It seems the trail of kerosene, judging by the way the fire spread, either ended or began at your hotel door, Mr. Trehune."

Sampson frowned, then signed, "Or Claire Fletcher's, since her room was just across the hall. Or Voisin's, just down the hall?"

Hodges nodded as Abel repeated Sampson's thoughts.

116

"About Voisin, Mr. Trehune. The desk clerk states that he saw Voisin running down the staircase into the lobby—fully clothed, mind you—shouting to beat all hell. It was Voisin who first alerted the hotel staff, and allowed the switchboard operator to warn the guests. Because of him, I guess there were no other deaths."

"So? We should give him a medal," Sampson signed. Abel censored the flippancy from Sampson's remarks, but relayed their substance to Hodges, who agreed.

"There is still a point or two which isn't clear, though. It seems that Voisin cannot account for most of yesterday afternoon, and all of last night. Says he was in his room part of the time, preparing a statement he planned on making at his contempt hearing. He didn't feel like answering the phone or the door, he says, because he doesn't like interruptions when he's thinking."

"So who does?" signed Sampson impatiently.

"The rest of the time, he maintains, he was out. Just out walking. He didn't stop anywhere and he doesn't think he spoke to anyone. Doesn't think he was seen by anyone, either. Just out walking."

"No crime," said Sampson, willing Hodges to get to the point, if indeed he had one.

"Show him," said Abel, and Hodges lifted a large envelope from his lap. He removed three photographs from the envelope, handed them to Sampson, and studied his reaction.

They were photographs, as Sampson saw from the stamp in red ink on the back of each, taken by the Office of the Medical Examiner, Hastings County, Hastings, Connecticut. The subject was the face of Claire Fletcher. It was a dead face, and again Sampson felt a deep sense of regret, of almost personal loss. He had enjoyed her, and that was something he could say of few people he had met in his life.

The photographs had been taken under bright laboratory

117

lights, which revealed the flaws in her face. Each was a close-up, a head shot. Each was taken from a different angle, but all were detailed, searching exposures of her face. They showed unmistakably that, beneath each eye, Claire Fletcher's cheeks had been marked, mutilated, as though she had been repeatedly stabbed with a needle. Sampson handed the photos back to Hodges, sickened by the sight of Fletcher's pock-marked face.

"So you see, Mr. Trehune, we have the doctor in custody and are holding him as a material witness. There are a few questions that need answering, don't you agree?"

Sampson agreed. There were many questions that desperately wanted answering. But probably not the ones the police were going to ask Voisin.

Hodges had Sampson repeat his account of the fire, taking more notes, asking more questions. Finally he said, "I guess that'll do it for now, Mr. Trehune. I sure do appreciate your help. Just one more thing. I'll try to remember to have an officer bring a typed copy of this statement over here for you to sign. In case I forget, though, I'd appreciate it if you'd stop by the police station and sign it before you leave town. Just a formality." Hodges gave the address of the police station and wished Sampson a speedy recovery. "The doctor says nothing much is wrong with you," he added jovially. "You should be up and about in a week."

A week. Ha! When Hodges left, Sampson signed to Abel, inquiring about his evening.

"I played chess most of the time. Mrs. Bannon's a wonderful hostess. You should have gone."

"How many games?"

"Three," Abel answered, surprised at his friend's interest in a subject he usually found dull. "Two with Altman and one with Bannon."

"Is either any good?"

"Morton Bannon is mediocre, but bizarre. Dick Altman is much more methodical, a reasonably good player. Develops his end game poorly, however."

"Was everyone around all night?"

His friend smiled and nodded. "Afraid you'll have to look elsewhere for the guilty party."

"That nurse, Harmon—or whatever her name is—too?"

"She hardly left Altman's side, kibitzing and chatting. She got a little distracting, to tell the truth."

"All night?"

"Morton Bannon was bringing the car around to the front of the house and we were on the Bannon's front steps when we heard the first sirens. We all drove to the hotel, and arrived just when the fire trucks did. The fire had a pretty good start by that time."

"You all drove?" Sampson's mind was racing, his fingers barely able to keep up with his thoughts.

"Yes, Mr. and Mrs. Bannon, Dick Altman, Nancy Harmon, and myself. It seemed a natural enough thing to do."

"Did you ride with Bannon?"

"No, as a matter of fact, Mr. and Mrs. Bannon left as soon as the sirens started. I rode with Altman and Nancy Harmon in Dick's car. But we followed them directly to the hotel. We never lost sight of them for a minute."

"Then what?"

"You do have a suspicious nature. Then we all—that is, Dick, Morton, and myself—pitched in and helped. Leading people out of the building and across the street, keeping bystanders away, administering a little necessary first aid. Morton even injured his hand slightly on a sliver of glass. To say nothing of his suit, which was ruined by smoke and water."

"Ah, so," spelled Sampson.

"Don't be foolish; none of them could have had anything to do with that fire, and you know it. And incidentally, before your lurid fascination for crime gets the better of you, both Hodges and Shaw are busy checking the whereabouts last night of the other physicians who were here last Sunday. So far, they've turned up nothing suspicious. Everyone seems accounted for, innocently."

"I need some clothes," Sampson signed.

Abel was actually shocked. "Clothes? But why? Surely you're not thinking of getting up. It'll be several days before you're well enough to resume—"

Sampson's waving hands stopped him before he got really wound up.

"At least another day or two," conceded the miffed Dr. Abel.

"B-u-l-l-s-h-i-t."

ELEVEN

Sampson was pissed. With each step along the drab road, he counted a grievance.

Claire Fletcher was dead.

Dr. Henri Voisin was being detained as a material witness. He was in no position to treat Sampson's deafness, even if Sampson overcame a sudden distrust of all sharp objects.

The death of Harrison Wolberg was as far as ever from being satisfactorily explained.

And one Sampson Trehune, a modest and retiring book appraiser who had just passed his forty-fourth birthday—this inoffensive, likable person had nearly been cremated!

The clothes he now wore—supplied by Abel, who, under protest, had visited the Hastings Men's Emporium—were adequate. That is, Sampson was in no danger of being arrested for indecent exposure. Beyond that, he was not sure. The trousers were stylish and very tight in the waist and crotch. Designed by eunuchs for eunuchs, he had thought while trying to zip the fly. By Hastings's standards, the shirt was undoubtedly stylish also, a long-sleeved sport shirt with wide pink stripes. The maroon jacket, made of some cheap synthetic material, had the kind of brass buttons he despised.

The clumsy-looking shoes, square-toed, ugly brown, with raised heels of some sort, were even worse. He had taken only a dozen steps down the corridor of the clinic when the left shoe pinched his little toe, a warning of what was to come. It came sooner than expected. Too nervous to wait for the elevator—one had stopped at his floor, but it contained a man on a bed with tubes running into his nose, mouth, and arm— he tried the stairs. By the time he reached the ground floor, the right shoe had started to work on his heel.

The disposable toothbrush and disposable razor he had used had left, respectively, a tuft between his teeth and several nicks on his neck and chin.

Then the head-nurse-*cum*-harpy had behaved rudely. Sampson had insisted upon leaving the Altman Clinic, and she had insisted upon his staying, regaling him with all the gory details of what surely would happen to him the moment he walked out the front door. He kept nodding until her pitch was finished, and signed a release anyway.

She had undoubtedly telephoned his lack of character and his moral turpitude to the cashier, for when he stopped as instructed, the purple-haired woman regarded him with disapproval, casting little sidelong glances at him while she shuffled papers and spoke into the telephone. Obviously Samp-

121

son was disreputable. He had no money to pay his bill. He had no hospital insurance card, or at the very least a policy coverage number. And he had no identification!

A personal appearance by Dr. Richard Altman had been necessary to secure Sampson's release. Even then there had been problems, since Altman had tried to convince him that his health demanded a longer stay in the clinic. Sampson believed that his health might depend upon his getting out of it. Altman finally gave in.

"What about some money?" Sampson had signed to Abel when the doctor had dropped off the clothes.

"Money?"

"Yes. You know, that green stuff."

Abel checked his wallet. "Here," he said, handing Sampson a bill.

"Ten dollars!" Very generous. "As I recall, you owe me something like four hundred."

"Beside the point. I'm short of cash. Anyway, what do you need money for? Everything's going to be done for you—meals, lodging. You have a decent pair of pants, a shirt, even a jacket. What more do you want? The ten is more than enough for cigarettes and magazines. Any more and you might get into trouble. See you."

So, Altman having smoothed the way, Sampson approached the purple-haired harridan about cashing a personal check. She was properly aghast. People can't even pay their bills, yet they want to cash checks. Still, the doctor had guaranteed Sampson's solvency.

"Do you have your checkbook?" she demanded grimly.

"No . . . the fire . . ." he answered politely. She glared at him as if that hardly constituted a decent excuse. "Blank check?" he inquired humbly.

"We're not supposed to cash them unless they've got those funny little numbers printed up in the corner. It'll probably

122

be returned to us. But I suppose that Dr. Altman would agree . . ."

Sampson began writing the name of his bank and the amount on the blank check when the cashier's eyes opened wide. "Under no circumstances can we cash a check for more than twenty dollars. Never." He had torn up the blank and started again.

Yes, Sampson was pissed.

And, he discovered, hungry. With the grand sum of thirty dollars in his pocket, he searched the road for a place to eat. The clinic's food had been out of the question, and with the Blue Coat Hotel in cinders, the only decent restaurant in town was gone. When he flopped down in a creaky wooden booth in a "Home Cooking Every Day" diner—favored, he had been told, by the clinic's personnel—he glowered. A menu appeared in front of him and, after glancing over it and sniffing, he unthinkingly ordered the Friday Special. His voice, he knew instantly, was all wrong. The young, pasty-faced waitress, strands of dishwater-blond hair falling over her perspiring brow, reared back as if some creation of Frankenstein had suddenly invaded the premises.

He gave up trying to talk, took the pencil from her hand, and neatly circled a soup, salad, the Friday Special, coffee, and milk on the menu. He held it up under her nose. She said something he couldn't see, jerked the menu from his hands, and flounced back to the lunch counter. She copied his order on her pad and, with great show, accompanied by other un-heard comments, erased his circles from the menu.

Sampson picked up a paper wedged in a corner of the booth and reread the details of the previous night's fire. Re-minded of the ordeal, his shoulder started to ache, his back, his ankle—not to mention the most recent casualty, his feet. He could almost taste the acrid smoke.

Finally, the Friday Special was placed in front of him and

with sinking heart Sampson examined it: minuscule fish fillets buried in a deep-fry batter and surrounded by greasy French fries and a defeated mound of coleslaw. He ate hungrily and got heartburn. Because he had nothing smaller, he left a five-dollar bill on the table, although the total meal was just $1.39. Give them something else to talk about, he thought, and left quickly.

He walked the three blocks back to the clinic and, stopping at the admitting desk again, suffered the stares of the purple-haired dragon. "Taxicab," he scribbled on the back of a yellow admission form and handed it to her, looking expectant and trying to seem both pleasant and reasonably helpless. She nodded curtly and disappeared into her glass cage. He watched as she raised the phone and spoke. She replaced the receiver and went about her regular chores of shuffling paper and tormenting the newly recovered with duns. After a minute, she looked at Sampson, almost as an afterthought, and mouthed something at him, managing to distort her words beyond recognition. Then she held up five fingers, repeated the motion, and accurately mouthed "minutes." Bravo.

Sampson trooped out the double doors and paced back and forth along the clinic's cinder driveway, determinedly ignoring his feet. After ten minutes, a battered pink-and-black Chevrolet of uncertain vintage pulled up and he got in. The driver was the same ancient, toothless one who had driven him and Abel to the clinic the Sunday before. "Hastings," Sampson barked. The driver turned and said something indecipherable. "Hastings," he repeated. "Town." Looking irritated, the ancient one pulled away.

I am such a gentle person, Sampson philosophized to himself, except when enraged.

When they chugged past the presumed lodging for a night of the illustrious George Washington, Sampson grunted. They were actually approaching the town proper, and that was the first thing which had gone right all day. Sampson reached over the seat and tapped the ancient one on the shoulder, indicating he should stop. Sampson handed him another of the five-dollar bills, and the old man shook his head. Probably can't change it, Sampson thought and, waving away the driver's protestations, he got out. He walked a few steps before a hand grabbed his arm. The ancient one, red-faced and mouthing indignantly, stood clutching him. People stopped and stared. The driver was holding up both hands, eight fingers, and gesticulating wildly in Sampson's face. He smelled of cheap whiskey.

That's right, Sampson recalled, they had crossed a township or city line. Wearily he waved the other's hands down, and forked over another five-dollar bill. Barely mollified, the ancient one walked away, not even making the pretense of giving change.

Ah, yes, the joys of small-town living, Sampson reflected, and resumed walking. For four blocks, he trudged through signs of decay: a vacant storefront, formerly a drugstore which had probably moved out of the center of Hastings to be near the Altman Clinic; a flyblown double window display in a cheap variety store; a furniture store promising three rooms of elegance for just one hundred dollars down; a clothing store with the latest of last year's designs in its windows, overpriced at that; another clothing store, proclaiming unimaginable bargains in the latest styles—styles which the outside world had written off as failures.

He wasn't even sure where he was headed. Aimlessly, he turned right at the next corner. Down at the end of the street were the ruins of the Blue Coat Hotel. An occasional wisp of smoke was visible, or was that just his imagination? He paused for a moment. Why not, he thought, and walked purposefully ahead.

But there wasn't much to see. He certainly should have

known that, he chided himself. A uniformed policeman patrolled the area's perimeter, from parking lot littered with broken glass and bits of wreckage to the hosed-down, swept-up street and back again. He kept away the curious, with their dangerous passion for souvenirs. The remains of the hotel bore no resemblance to any structure intended by man, except, perhaps, a piece Sampson had seen on a visit to the Museum of Modern Art.

Sampson was still pissed. The diner's food and the sight of the Blue Coat raised an unbearable taste in his throat. He felt frustrated because he didn't know what he wanted to do. But no use standing around. He turned back down the street and became conscious of the ugly shoe rubbing against his heel. He found a drugstore in the middle of the next block, one that was still struggling to survive. He picked up a small box of Band-Aids, accepted $4.70 in change, and refused a bag, tugging the box from the clerk's unwilling fingers.

He continued walking until he came to a neon sign that for some reason was winking on and off in the afternoon sun. "Harry's Place," it said. He headed for the Gents where he put a Band-Aid on his irritated heel. When he came back to the barroom, he discovered he was the only customer.

He sat near the door, absorbed in his own thoughts, and took a moment to register that a double Scotch-on-the-rocks had appeared before him, unordered. Leaning on the bar, dressed now in a more homely apron, pencil in one hand and racing form in the other, was the nameless bartender from the Blue Coat Lounge. Didn't waste much time, Sampson thought, and said so. "Good bartender, he can always get work, like that," the man said, snapping his fingers.

Leaning closer, he confided to Sampson, "Alas was scratched again today. I smell something." Sampson nodded sagely and swallowed, enjoying the burning, purifying liquor as it cleansed his throat. When it hit his stomach, however, it roused memories of his lunch, and he almost became ill again.

In a talkative mood, the bartender began to discuss the tragedy of the night before. "I hear the police are investigating, which must mean it wasn't no accident, right?"

Sampson shrugged and pointed to his empty glass.

"Double?"

Sampson nodded; the bartender poured.

"Sometimes—like now, you know—I wonder if we should have a woman in the county prosecutor's office. I mean, I know Belinda Shaw's smart as they come, but still, when something like this happens—well, I just don't know, y'know?" Sampson nodded. "I mean she's honest and all, and she's done some good things for Hastings, for the whole county. Like when she got the goods on those contractors who was padding the bills for the highway extension. Still, a woman's a woman."

Sampson, recalling Shaw's delightful round crimson lips, and the way she had of pronouncing words with "th" in them, murmured, "A woman," and nodded again.

"See, you know what I mean," the bartender said. "You think that foreign guy did it? I mean that doctor nut with the needles? I hear they got him locked up. And to think Marge, over at the bookstore—she had some of his books on her shelves. Right here in Hastings, that guy's stuff. Authors are all nuts probably anyway, right? And this guy was in Red China? Yeah, I bet he did it, huh? What do you think?"

"Could be," Sampson answered flatly, not sure of precisely what he did think at the moment.

The bartender was not to be put off, though. Probably a nervous reaction to the fire, Sampson speculated. "Were you there, in fire?" Sampson asked. The man shook his head, and picked up a towel, wiping the bar the full length. Sampson couldn't catch all his words, but gathered that the lounge

127

closed at midnight on Thursday nights, and that the man had taken just under a half-hour checking out his register and locking up the stock. Since the fire didn't start until . . .

"Sorry about your friend," the man said, his face showing real sympathy. "Funny how sometimes you just never know what to do or what's going to happen. Like, I may have been the very last person she ever spoke to on this earth, and because it was closing time and I had to meet this girl later and like that, you know, I was real short with her."

"She come back?" Sampson asked, interested.

"She never left," replied the bartender, settling in place against the back bar directly opposite Sampson. "Let's see, you left, and about five minutes later Belinda Shaw left. And so your lady friend, she was all alone at the table, you know? And then she gets this phone call—gee, I don't know, ten, ten-thirty, somewhere around there—and she has another martini. Boy, could she belt them things down."

Sampson got up, walked down the length of the bar, snared a bowl of pretzels, and returned to his stool. "She stayed?"

"Yeah, and she kept jumping up and down, going out to the lobby looking for whoever it was called her, I guess. Made me nervous."

"House phone or outside call?"

"Outside. Didn't have no house phone direct to the bar. Had to ring room service and get the bellhop out front and he gets the order. Guess they were afraid of losing tips or something if it went straight to the bar, you know?"

Sampson grunted, and thought a moment. "Man called?" he asked.

"Who else? Can't imagine that broad—sorry—that woman being so anxious over no other chick. She sure had a hungry look in her eyes. I don't go for that type, you know?"

"Did he ever show?" Sampson asked casually, after munching pretzels in a studied show of nonchalance.

128

"Naaw! That's what I was telling you. He kept calling, maybe every fifteen, twenty minutes, you know. And then when closing time rolls around, he ain't there yet, and I tell her kind of rough that she's gotta leave. I don't wanna speak ill of the dead, but that broad sure had some mouth on her, and she used it when I told her she couldn't wait at the bar."

"She leave?"

"She took her drink and sat on a chair, near the entrance to the restaurant, you know. That's the last I saw of her. Sitting, drinking, and waiting. You know, I bet he never did show up, and that poor woman was sitting waiting. I bet I was maybe the last person in the world she really talked to, and I was mean to her."

"Second to last," Sampson said softly, and left another five-dollar bill on the bar, hoping that it would cover two double Scotches and leave a few cents for a tip. It seemed to, for the bartender nodded his thanks and returned to the racing form.

As he slid off the bar stool and walked out into the October afternoon, Sampson had the germ of an idea. He was so pleased with himself that even the dreary fronts of Hastings were tolerable. But after another block, he wasn't sure any longer. He wasn't even sure of his own legal status. Would he be forced to stay in Hastings? If so, since the only hotel in town was a water-soaked pile of twisted, blackened metal and masonry, where was he to spend the night—or nights, God forbid?

If Voisin was innocent of killing Fletcher, then Sampson had hesitations about spending the night under almost any roof in Hastings. Whoever killed Claire Fletcher, and almost got him, that person might try again—in fact, almost certainly would try again. The stakes must be larger than Sampson imagined, for apparently the killer had not been bothered by all the innocent lives endangered in the hotel fire. Surely he

129

wouldn't pause at getting rid of one book appraiser from New York.

Lieutenant Hodges needed his signature on the statement relating what he could remember of last night's fire. Might as well get it over with, thought Sampson as he got his directions and set off toward the police station on Pleasant Street. A misnomer that, without doubt.

He passed Marge's Bookstore, paused by habit to glance at the window display, and moved on. Half a block later, he retraced his steps and entered the shop. A couple of children had their noses pressed against a glass case, debating the merits of licorice over chewing gum. A teen-ager was furtively flipping throught the magazine section, standing directly below a hand-lettered sign which read "Adult Readers Only." The lad seemed disappointed as he feverishly turned the pages.

But Sampson was in luck. There, between a salacious and poorly written best-selling novel and a volume on crocheting, was the book in the red-and-white dust jacket he sought. He removed the last copy of *Acupuncture Today* from the shelf. He paid for it, reluctantly handing seven dollars to a sour little lady with purple hair. Must be inbreeding, he thought, a unique matching of chromosomes to produce just that shade of purple. Or maybe it's something in the Connecticut air. He accepted his change—one nickel—and added it to the two crumpled bills and two quarters and two dimes in his pocket. His total fortune, he considered moodily—all that stood between him and destitution. *Destitute in Hastings*—title for a book? Bad title. Probably a bad book, too.

As he turned a corner two blocks later, he saw the police station. Even without a sign, it had to be the place. The solitary building was a red brick box, two stories, with a white concrete façade and fake columns holding up nothing. There were shrubberies for criminals to hide in. Even in summer, the grass probably looked sickly.

130

Inside, behind a partition with sliding glass windows, sat the epitome of the small-town policeman. He was a sergeant, tall, with one-time muscles gone to fat, and his paunch embraced the edge of the metal desk as he tried to look efficient. He was florid, and might have been described as cherubic, if such a building could be said to harbor angels of any degree. He was busily tapping his pencil on the desk blotter, apparently keeping time to a song coming from a small black-and-silver transistor perched on the overflowing "in" basket.

In as capable a voice he could muster, Sampson asked for Lieutenant Hodges. "Ain't here now" came the helpful reply. Back to tapping the pencil. Once again, Sampson, watching the pencil and imagining the music, felt blessed in not hearing.

"My name's Trehune," Sampson offered, speaking directly at the bobbing head, which now matched the pencil's tempo. "Supposed to sign a statement. The fire."

The sergeant—a permanent rank, no doubt, for even with the retirement or death of every other person on the force, he would not move higher—the sergeant sighed, lifted his bulk from the chair, fluttering the papers in the "in" basket as he did so, pulled up his belt, and lumbered over to a file cabinet. He opened it and went patiently through its contents. Finally he closed the file drawer, stood irresolutely for a moment, then padded across the room and entered a frosted-glass door marked "PRIVATE." He came back holding some papers in his ham hand. "Sampson Trehune?" he asked suspiciously.

"Yeah," Sampson croaked impatiently.

"Note from the lieutenant says you can't talk. Funny." He eased down into his chair and shoved the pencil into his mouth.

"I can talk a little," Sampson said.

"Unhuh," the man grunted, or something like that, his lips moving but making no identifiable pattern. "Well, I guess it's

O.K. You got anything to identify yourself with, Mr. Trehune?"

"No," Sampson answered wearily. "Fire," he repeated, this time forming his hands into a mime of flickering flames.

For a moment, the sergeant seemed mesmerized, watching Sampson's undulating hands. Then he nodded: "Yeah, yeah, I guess that's right." He scratched his head, then said officially, "O.K., Mr. Trehune, now do you have anything to add to what you told the lieutenant this morning?"

Sampson shook his head.

The sergeant nodded again.

"The lieutenant said I had to sign it," Sampson said.

"Well, Mr. Trehune, we thought you'd be in the hospital for a few days and we haven't got your statement typed up quite yet."

"Could you type it now? Should get back to New York."

"New York, huh?"

"I live there."

"Yeah, well, now, let's see. I can type this, sure enough, but I don't know if you should hurry down and catch the next train. Not until the Assistant Prosecutor—that's Miss Shaw, you know—gets a handle on this Blue Coat mess. It's not that you're under arrest or anything, but just to keep things tidy-like. Understand?"

Sampson nodded, and the sergeant pulled up a typewriter on a metal table and made a face. The wheel probably screeched; served him right. He rolled a piece of official stationery and three carbons into the machine, examined his two forefingers carefully, straightened his shoulders, then hunched suddenly down over the typewriter, turning his back on Sampson, who sat waiting on the hard slatted bench.

After a few moments, the head of the sergeant became visible again, then his paunch, as he rose and crumpled the paper, carbons and all, into a ball and lobbed it into a waste-

132

basket. He glanced sourly at Sampson, took out more paper and carbons, and started again.

Sampson, after the second set of paper and carbons had been discarded, approached the sergeant, borrowed a pencil, and wrote in block letters, "VOISIN."

"What about him?"

"Could I see him?" Sampson wrote.

"Well, I don't know."

Sampson held up the book he carried and gestured.

"You wanna give him that, huh?" The sergeant took the book, examined it as if making a search for concealed weapons, seemed disappointed. "What's he want to read his own book for?"

Sampson shook his head, opened the book, and pretended to write on the flyleaf.

A few seconds of incomprehension. Then, "Autograph, huh? Strange, but I guess it's all right. It'll take me awhile to get this here statement of yours typed up anyway." He led Sampson down a brightly lit corridor, and paused before a metal door at the end. Taking a key ring from his pocket, the sergeant negotiated the door. They went into a room, where the man told Sampson to wait, going out himself by a second door, which he closed securely behind him. The room where Sampson was seemed barren enough: a table and four wooden chairs, a plastic ashtray, tile floor, institutional green cinder-block walls, slight but pervasive smell of disinfectant, no windows. A row of lights crossed the ceiling, illuminating everything in their glare.

TWELVE

When the sergeant led Voisin in, Sampson stood up. He was startled by the doctor's appearance. On the surface he looked a mess. He was dressed in the suit he had worn the Sunday before; his shirt was wilted, tie askew, hair tousled. But despite lines of weariness around his eyes and mouth and an over-all impression of haggardness, his bearing was erect and full of command. He motioned Sampson to the chair across the table from him as he slowly sat down himself. The motion spoke volumes, a host warmly welcoming a guest but apologizing for his surroundings.

The sergeant stopped at the door, still apparently unsure, and Voisin dismissed him with a look. The man left, locking the door behind him.

"Well, Mr. Trehune, I am surprised indeed to see you again. Forgive me if I am not more hospitable, but under the circumstances . . ." Voisin left his sentence uncompleted and shrugged. Sampson nodded sympathetically. "You know, of course, these fools believe that I had something to do with the fire? That I, Henri Voisin, deliberately burned down that wretched hotel, killing Miss Fletcher."

Again Sampson nodded, and Voisin went on, becoming visibly more angry. "They have not said so, of course, but still they keep me here. Still they ask their stupid questions. I know what they are thinking. That I was frightened by what that woman would write about acupuncture. That I set a match to her skirts in order to silence her. Just because

134

I took a walk, because I cannot account for my every moment like some—like some—" Rage caused his words to fail and Sampson took the opportunity to speak.

Gathering every ounce of his oral skill, he told Voisin of his conversation with Lieutenant Hodges, of the questions which he had been asked, and of his memory of the awful moments when the fire reached his room.

Voisin nodded sadly. "I am so glad that you escaped, Mr. Trehune. And equally sorry that the poor woman was trapped." Sampson was surprised, for quite obviously the police had not told Voisin all the details surrounding the death of Claire Fletcher. Slowly, his voice slipping out of control, Sampson sketched in the results of the autopsy. "Smothered, or choked. Not by fire or smoke."

Voisin became interested. "So. So. Does that prove that I had anything to do with it?"

"More. Her face." Sampson opened Voisin's book to the flyleaf and drew, with a cheap ballpoint he had filched from his clinic room, a crude picture of a human face. Then, as carefully as possible, Sampson dotted in the needle scars which the Medical Examiner's photograph of the dead woman had revealed. Nearly a dozen on each cheek.

Voisin seemed hypnotized as he pondered the implications. "*La piqûre morte,*" he said finally, and Sampson agreed. "Now, now I see. Someone was attempting to kill her with a needle. He was searching for the precise place where a single needle insertion can reverse the meridian's flow, can cause death. But such a puncture would not show death caused by suffocation; even the primitives who call themselves doctors could see that."

"Couldn't find the right point," Sampson said. "This time."

Voisin did not take long to appreciate the significance of Sampson's last remark. "Wolberg. Of course. Wolberg. That

135

would explain the pulses I discovered after death. That would explain everything." The agitated Frenchman kicked his chair back and broke for the door.

"Wait!" Sampson yelled, or hoped he did. Whatever came out, Voisin froze.

"But why? We must tell the police. Without delay. Now perhaps they will stop hounding me and do their job."

"Wait," Sampson repeated.

Voisin now stood opposite him, and some of his anger was directed toward Sampson. "Why wait?"

"Proof."

"But of course I can prove it. Such information, about the forbidden points—it has been available, if little discussed, for hundreds of years. I could tell them."

Sampson waved him silent. "Who would believe?"

"I'll make them believe!" mouthed Voisin adamantly.

"More still." And Sampson opened Voisin's book to the flyleaf, where his sketch of Claire Fletcher's pocked face stared at them. He handed Voisin the pen, and said, "Autograph."

Voisin gaped. "Now? An autograph? After what has happened, you can think of such foolishness! You are a book collector, I remember, and perhaps if Henri Voisin scribbles his name your book becomes more valuable. But—"

"Sign."

Voisin puffed his cheeks in exasperation and resigned himself to indulging the man opposite him, as if he were a child or a loony. He jerked the pen from Sampson with his right hand, and held down the page of the book. Sampson reached over and stopped his wrist just as the doctor was about to write.

"Real name," he said, staring directly into Voisin's eyes. Voisin shrugged off Sampson's grip and tried to pass off the words he had just heard. Sampson repeated them, holding the man just as forcefully with his gaze. "Real name!" Voisin tried to look puzzled, then indignant, but it didn't quite come off. Sampson saw his neck muscles tighten, his hand freeze for a second as it hovered over the book, his body suddenly stiffen. A barely perceptible movement of withdrawal followed.

"What did you say?" Voisin asked.

"Your real name." Sampson knew his bluff had worked, even though the man, now back in control of himself, executed the careless shrug of the injured Frenchman. He was good, but not quite good enough. The two stared at each other for a moment, and Voisin began very lightly to perspire. Beads dotted his forehead and his upper lip, around his unkempt mustache.

"The truth," Sampson resumed.

"Just what is it you want, Mr. Trehune?"

"Truth."

Voisin now attempted to look bemused, but only succeeded in looking guilty.

"Fletcher thought she knew truth," Sampson wrote, hating to mar the dust jacket, even on the inside. "Maybe that's why she was killed. She was going to tell all today."

Voisin returned to his seat and shook his head sadly. "So she could not let the past remain buried. She thought she had found the truth. Perhaps. But believe me, Mr. Trehune, that was not why she was killed. Nor did I kill her. You must believe that."

"I do. Maybe."

Voisin leaned toward Sampson, his elbows resting on the table which separated them. "Assume for a moment that this truth which you so determinedly seek, Mr. Trehune, suppose that it does exist. What then? It is but one of many truths. How important is this one truth? Suppose it has nothing to do, this truth, with Fletcher's or Wolberg's death? Then what?

"Consider my position, Mr. Trehune. My passport has been taken, but I have been assured by the French Embassy in Washington that it will be returned to me and I will be free to travel just as soon as this business is cleared up. I mean this foolishness about insulting the august judge. I am sure now that, regardless of their suspicions, no one can prove I had anything to do with any other crime. So. In a few days, I shall be gone, out of the country, and back to China to continue my work.

"Do you know, Mr. Trehune, that acupuncture points may actually exist inside of the body, on the internal organs themselves? Think what that could mean—think of the reduction in deaths resulting from radical surgery if such points can be proven to exist and their functions understood.

"Yes, I shall go about my business, which is curing people. What of this truth which you seek then, Mr. Trehune? Which is more important, sir, this truth or the truth that says with certainty that you will someday hear again?"

A long, drying speech. Voisin took a small tin container from his pocket, opened it, and offered it to Sampson. "Your throat must be dry, too. This room. The fire. Your nerves. Relax, Mr. Trehune. Have a pastille."

Sampson took two, and thought Voisin was pleased. They tasted and smelled of violets. Voisin continued, obviously in no hurry to get back to the subject at hand. "The fools were not going to let me keep them, afraid I would poison myself," he said, chuckling. "Fortunately, Miss Shaw, an admirable woman, assured them that pastilles are candy. They have always been my favorite. They remind me of my childhood."

"Your birthplace?"

Voisin inhaled deeply and slumped in his chair. "Where I was born is of no importance. When the Western interest in needle therapy was born, and when it was first studied seriously—these facts are important. Do you naïve, suddenly awakened Americans believe needles were not used by European practitioners before? Why, for nearly half a century French and German physicians have been seriously experimenting—"

"On whom?"

Fear showed in Voisin's eyes. "What do you mean?"

"Experimenting on whom?"

"You, too, Mr. Trehune?" Voisin sat gloomily silent. Finally he began again. "Of all the afflictions which rack the human body, perhaps the saddest is aging. The degeneration of tissue disturbs the mind as well as the body. For this, even the needles can do nothing. To witness the daily disintegration of a human life—that is tragic, Mr. Trehune."

Sampson said nothing, just stared. Voisin stared back. "So?" said Sampson impatiently.

The doctor seemed to be debating with himself, then looked up, smiling. "Let me tell you a story, Mr. Trehune. A sad story, but one with perhaps a happy ending sometime. And you must remember that this story takes place a long time ago, and in another country."

Henri Voisin crossed his legs, folded his arms behind his head, and stared at a point above and beyond Sampson. "There was once a man, a very good man—a brilliant man, even—who led a busy and productive life, and who aged, perhaps not easily but happily, into what is known as senility. On that day in June, 1940, when the Nazis entered Paris, this man was nearly eighty years old. Remember that, Mr. Trehune. Nearly eighty years old." Voisin wagged his head at Sampson, underscoring his last words.

"This man was a doctor, trained in the best Western tradition at the Université de Paris. Scientific curiosity and anguish over his helplessness when faced by human suffering caused

139

him to search into the corners of man's knowledge. He discovered a small German society devoted to acupuncture, called something like the Gold Needle Society. After nearly three decades, this doctor realized his dream. In a small town about fifty kilometers from Paris, he opened a clinic, which combined the practice of Western with Eastern medicine.

"In 1940 the Boche came, and they occupied his clinic, using it for their own purposes. This old man continued to make his daily appearances at the clinic, happily caring for a few of his older patients. He never knew to what purpose the Germans used the needles and his rooms. The clinic developed a reputation, not a pretty one. The appearance of the Gestapo in 1942, when the Resistance became stronger, virtually condemned the clinic and its founder. People who had been his friends called him beast."

Voisin paused, and repeated again, "Yes. Beast. An eighty-two-year-old, senile monster." Sampson said nothing, both fascinated by the story and afraid to break Voisin's reverie.

"This man's son, however, knew what was being done to him, and used his position to work secretly with the underground. No one ever knew about that. And when the Allies drove the Germans out and occupied France themselves, this old man was murdered by a mob. Executed, they say, but the trial was a mockery. It was murder.

"And his son? He barely escaped with his life. Through a friend in the underground, he was furnished with a membership card in the Communist Party and told to flee to the East, where he would be safe with a new name, at least for a while.

"Justice was quick in those bad days, Mr. Trehune, and few people argued over the fine points. Snap judgments meant the difference between life and death. So the young man accepted a new identity and later slipped into the Eastern sector of Germany. He enrolled at the University of Leipzig, with little difficulty achieving high marks in medicine."

Voisin struggled, searching for the right words. "One thing this young man had learned as a child from his father. There are just two things of importance in life, two things worth doing well. Making love, and knowing the truth. After all, he was a French boy, Mr. Trehune. With the aid of a student or two from outside Germany, this boy pursued the very practice that had so disgraced his father, a new kind of medicine called needle therapy."

Voisin paused and meticulously opened the small tin box. He removed another pastille and placed it in his mouth. "As he studied, he became convinced that there was actually some truth, a great deal of truth, in this ancient art. But the bureaucrats at Leipzig were not interested in truth, only in producing more trained doctors in the least possible time. They were desperate. Who could blame them? Germany had suffered terrible casualties, and the Cold War idiocy had drained off even more promising young men.

"So the young man left Leipzig before completing his final year and returned to the West. There, thanks to the Cold War, he was hailed as a defector to freedom, given new papers in his adopted name and a few hundred marks. Then he was ignored. Again he tried to pursue his newly discovered truth, but at the time, even in West Germany, the schools were not interested, seeing it as either a Communist plot or a throwback to witchcraft. As the young man grew older, money became harder to get, and he was frozen out of medicine. People even asked questions about his origin.

"Then, in a small town near Rhinestaddt, a fortuitous happening. The sleepy little community had only one doctor, a recent university graduate, and he was killed when his car overturned. Our young man was present and tried to save the doctor's life. The body was removed to an undertaker, and that evening a thief broke into the cottage where the doctor

141

had lived by himself, and ransacked it. The authorities investigated, found nothing, and dropped the case.

"But our young man now had a fresh identity, and a diploma from a German university. He finally reached China, where the expulsion of the Nationalists meant the revitalization of traditional medicine. He studied, he practiced, he learned. Finally, he was certain that his pursuit was worth all the troubles it had caused him. He had proven that acupuncture could significantly reduce man's suffering.

"An interesting story, Mr. Trehune, is it not?"

Sampson nodded. Eventually he asked, "But what about Wolberg?"

"What about him? He is dead. Beyond any help."

"Not just dead. Murdered."

Voisin shrugged. "Even in this marvelous country of yours, thousands die from lack of proper medical attention. Is that not also murder?"

Sampson rubbed his eyes, then blinked them rapidly. He made himself exercise them: up, down, left, right. They felt gritty, and burned when the tears started.

"But I feel I have tired you with my childish little tale, Mr. Trehune. My imagination sometimes is so vivid. After this silly misunderstanding with the judge is over, we can talk again."

Still Sampson said nothing.

"Well, what would you have me do, Mr. Trehune?" Nervously, Voisin took another pastille and savored it, staring down at his shoes.

Sampson took two, chewed, and almost broke a tooth. He swallowed, then explained to Voisin just what he thought they should do.

Voisin's objections were cut short by the arrival of the sergeant. "You all finished?"

Sampson nodded, but just before Voisin was led back to his cell, he asked another question. "Your English. Perfect. Where did you learn?"

Voisin smiled. "I still have some secrets, Mr. Trehune."

When the sergeant reappeared, he was sucking his right index finger. He ran the fingers of his left hand through his hair. The gesture made Sampson focus on the sergeant's forehead, smudged with carbon. A ton of paper in the trash can, Sampson thought. Wouldn't it be cheaper to hire a secretary? Actually, Sampson didn't feel critical. If the sergeant had been an expert typist, Sampson would never have heard Voisin's tale.

"Got your statement typed. You can sign it now," the sergeant announced when they returned to the desk. "I haven't been able to get ahold of Miss Shaw on the telephone. Guess you'll have to stay around for a while longer."

"Pleasure," said Sampson. "Town growing on me."

The sergeant studied him for a moment, then returned to his radio.

Outside, Sampson sucked in fresh air before setting off for Harry's Place. Shaking his head sadly to the bartender's offer of another Scotch, he asked him to call a cab.

"Bannon Electronics," he instructed the toothless one as he climbed into the Chevrolet.

The first stop was a letdown, a complete bust. The watchman who finally answered the insistent honkings of the cab was firm.

"Strict orders," he said, standing in a pool of weird but clarifying light. "Sorry, Mister, but nobody's around. Mr. Bannon was very explicit. Since we got those defense contracts, we keep security real tight." The man smiled to himself, recalling a joke. "Why, this new stuff is so secret that even the fellows working here aren't allowed to know what's going on." Sampson refused the guard's offer to call Mr. Bannon at home and have him O.K. Sampson's entry.

"Gum," said Sampson. He didn't like the taste of violets, after all.

"Eh?"

"Gum. Gum!"

The watchman pointed in the direction of a small store which stood a block away from the plant's main gate.

"Gum," Sampson said, at the store, to the stooped little man in a soiled white apron. The man searched anxiously around, then yelled something at the open door leading to the rear of the store. He must have got a reply, since he went to the shelf below a typewriter.

"Only here in the evenings, don't know the stock so well," he explained as Sampson handed him a quarter. As the man rang up the sale, Sampson looked around the small store. His distaste at what he saw must have been evident. The man apologized.

"Ain't much to look at, I admit. But it keeps the wife busy and sure helps pay the bills. Especially since the plant started laying off and slowing down. I had seniority. Nearly twenty years. Even me, I was down to just two days a week."

Embarrassed, Sampson pocketed his change and tried to think of something pleasant and encouraging to say. "Business picking up soon."

"Sure will, thank God. We need it. The whole town needs it. We'll be getting in fresh stock next week, probably paint the place, too. Get rid of all this junk." His right arm indicated dingy glass cases filled with candy, gloves, cheap jewelry, batteries, and two-dollar radios. On top of one case rested a box lid containing dusty odds and ends. Propped up between a wind-up toy automobile and a soiled yellow lady's wallet was a sign written in a shaky hand: "SPECIAL! HALF PRICE." The man kept talking, but Sampson ignored him. He

144

grabbed the box and rummaged through its contents. He came up with four small pocket-size notebooks. Each had a familiar spotting on its orange cover.

"These. How much?"

"Half price. Half of sixty cents. That'll be thirty cents. Plus two cents tax. Yep. A kid spilled a bottle of Coke on the counter about a month ago, and these got damaged. One of the risks in dealing with the public, you know."

Sampson handed him a dollar and waited for his change. "Sell the rest?"

"Yep. About a week ago, maybe two. Some city fellow who was doing something over at the plant. He seemed kinda nervous. Didn't mind the stains at all. Saw him the next day, scribbling away. I remember, he was so busy scribbling that he tripped over a forklift."

Sampson smiled and shook his head while he struggled to find something to say to keep the conversation going. Not that he really needed to know anything more. At last, he ordered a hero sandwich. There was a pause, then the man's wife appeared and grudgingly began constructing the sandwich.

"Looks good," he volunteered, trying to seem interested as the dumpy woman piled cheese, lettuce, some stale-looking cold cuts, and a tomato slice onto the roll. "Must get lots orders from plant," he said. She looked at him strangely. "Accident," he said, and she stared at him as he pointed inanely to his throat and ears. Then she went back to the sandwich. "Know Bannon's secretary?" Sampson asked, turning his attention to the husband.

"Doesn't have one. Not a real one, anyway. Ain't had a secretary since Harriet Stone left 'bout two years ago. She was a real looker," he added reminiscently; worry flicked across his face as he glanced at his wife.

145

"Hussy. Good riddance," she said. "Those kind never stay, and the town's better off without them." Then she turned and marched out, dropping Sampson's hero on the counter.

"That'll be eighty cents, plus four cents, makes eight-four cents," the man said swiftly as his customer lifted the sandwich.

Back in the cab, with the toothless one distorting his mouth. Whistling, probably. Sampson was not sure what to do next. "Altman Clinic," he said, and relaxed against the seat, toying with the sandwich. Then he changed his mind, and motioned for the driver to stop. "Here?" the man asked. They were in a sparsely populated area of Hastings—or, rather, of the unincorporated area just outside Hastings proper. "Well," the man said, annoyed. "Now what?"

A good question. Now what? Suddenly it dawned on him that he was really frightened. This was no longer a game. One wrong step and he would never hear again—nor see, touch, taste, or smell.

"Know where Belinda Shaw lives?" he asked.

The driver nodded impatiently. "The Shaws have lived in the same place for over three generations. Probably live there for three more. You wanna go there?"

"Hurry," said Sampson, and hoped she was home. He didn't have enough money to pay the fare.

THIRTEEN

It was 9:30 when Belinda Shaw, Dr. Henri Voisin, and Sampson entered the luxurious Bannon living room. The Saturday night party to celebrate the return to full production at Bannon Electronics and the revitalization of Hastings's economy was in full swing. The three newcomers stood by the arched doorway for a moment, and Sampson noticed a ripple of turning heads as news of their presence spread. They were the center of attention.

"Belinda Shaw, what are you doing?" The speaker was Jesse Gimball, the County Prosecutor, who nearly upset his wife's drink as he rushed to confront them. "This is hardly the time—" He turned and said something Sampson couldn't see, but his face was flushed and he was probably shouting. Then he stared at Voisin and Sampson as though a pair of lepers had crashed the party. "What the hell are they doing here? Have you lost your mind? I—"

"Belinda, dear, how nice you could come. And Mr. Trehune. And this must be Dr. Voisin we've heard so much about." The perfect hostess, Constance Bannon had come gliding to the rescue. Taking their cue, the guests turned back to their conversations, cigarettes were lit, and people in progress to the bar continued on their way. Mrs. Bannon, elegant in a white satin blouse and black velvet palazzo pants, offered her creamy hand to Sampson and Voisin. The doctor bowed and raised the hand to his lips, apparently murmuring some Gallic compliment, for Mrs. Bannon smiled even more brilliantly and added a graceful little curtsy. "Why, sir, you are indeed a gentleman." She tucked her arm under his. "You simply must come and meet my other guests."

With Voisin out of the way, Gimball started in on Shaw again: "Now, Belinda, what could you be thinking of? On your own authority, you released that needle maniac for over six hours last night. I just found out about it this morning. Tonight—did you bring him here by yourself? Who gave you permission—"

"You did, Counselor, when you phoned me at 8 P.M. last Sunday and asked me to handle the little dustup at the Altman Clinic."

"But that was just one small matter. Now we've got the fire at the Blue Coat and the death of that reporter woman, and this thing is serious. It's a new ball game. I've known you all your life. You've always been reasonable. Now, use your head, girl."

Though she bridled visibly at the term "girl," she replied composedly, "It's the same game, Counselor. Murder—two of them."

"Now, you listen here, don't tell me you swallow that hogwash that crazy Frenchman's been spouting. Do you? . . . Well, *do* you?"

"Yes, I do."

Gone now was the last trace of Gimball's avuncular approach. "Is this some kind of trick you cooked up to get votes? Oh, yes, I know you plan to run against me next spring, and let me tell you, some of this is going to rub off on you. Our folks here don't take kindly to any fancy shenanigans. You better think twice. If there's any funny business going on, I'm not going to pick your chestnuts from the fire. Nosiree."

"Don't worry, I wouldn't ask you to. There's no way you can get your fingers burned."

Their exchange was interrupted by Dr. Abel, who merely looked at Sampson and said, "Well?"

Quickly Sampson signed, "Hi. Tell you about it later."

Abel, calm but aggrieved, signed, "I went to the hospital last night, and you weren't there. I left a message that the Bannons were gracious enough to have a room ready, but you —all you did was have someone call to say you were busy. Well?"

Gimball, beside himself with frustration, stormed, "What the hell are you saying?"

"Hello," said Sampson. "A word from French. Popular greeting after Norman Conquest. 1066." Gimball quivered, certain he was being made a fool of, but not certain how, nor what he should do about it. Shaw tactfully led him away, heading toward the bar at the far end of the room.

"Well?" asked Abel again.

"Thirsty? Let's get a drink," Sampson signed, and headed off to the bar.

"Scotch, rocks," Sampson told the uniformed bartender.

A hand grabbed his shoulder. "No drinking, Mr. Trehune. I will not treat patients who have ingested any drugs, and that certainly includes alcohol." Henri Voisin sported the undisguised smugness of the teetotaler. Anguished, Sampson put the untouched drink down on the bar, the tang of the untasted Scotch still in his nostrils. Voisin nodded his approval of this display of will power. He patted Sampson on the arm, and walked off, saying, "Soon. Soon."

Abel, his own drink freshened, tapped Sampson on the shoulder and signed, "What's all that about?" Sampson mournfully watched the retreating back of Henri Voisin. "Soda water," he told the bartender. He tipped about a teaspoon of his Scotch into it and raised the glass toward Abel. "To me and my ears. I may hear before the night's over. Well, drink up. Aren't you happy? After all, this was partly your idea. Here's to the sound and the fury. Like that? It's a joke." Abel just stared at Sampson and looked pained.

A second bartender had served Shaw and Gimball, who had disappeared into the crowd. Sampson caught a glimpse of them as they were joined by a third person. Mrs. Gimball, probably. I suppose he calls her "Mother," Sampson thought. Back toward the archway he saw his host for the first time; Morton Bannon, along with his wife, was evidently saying good-bye to a tubby man and his equally tubby wife.

"The Mayor," Abel signed. "You'd think Bannon was the Mayor," he added. The tubby man smiled and bowed, smiled and bowed.

149

His Honor's departure served as a signal. Gradually the guests began to leave. Just a dozen or so remained when Voisin dropped his bomb. "Perhaps you would like to see a demonstration of acupuncture?" There was a stunned silence. "Last Sunday, circumstances prevented me from treating Mr. Trehune for deafness. Perhaps now, if there are no objections . . ."

People were looking at each other, mouths agape. Gimball, beet red, rushed to Sampson with Belinda Shaw close behind. Previously he had been torn between leaving with the rest of the guests, which his wife favored, or staying on, since he was afraid he would miss something. "By God, no!" he shouted now, or at least Sampson assumed he shouted, since everyone in the room was looking at them. "Enough of this witch-doctor stuff has been going on around here without—"

"I think the choice is Mr. Trehune's," said Shaw.

"Like hell it is! This stuff is illegal, isn't it? Against the law, in case you remember what that means? Pull out one needle and, by God, I'll slap him in jail and throw away the key." The County Prosecutor looked around him as if he had given a signal for applause that misfired.

"It isn't quite that easy," Shaw continued. "Although you might prosecute after the fact, using the New York decision as a precedent, you would be hard put to prevent the act, since the charge is a state offense and the Connecticut courts have never ruled on acupuncture. They've never had a case."

"Thank God for that," Gimball said piously, but his eyes crinkled with a hint of worry. Law was not his strong suit.

Mrs. Bannon proved an unexpected ally. "Now, Jesse," she said companionably, "I'm sure I don't know anything about all this, but it's fascinating. And I know Henri wouldn't do anything dangerous." She smiled at the doctor.

"A most simple procedure."

"I'm all ears," said Sampson. A few nervous giggles.

"But it's illegal," insisted the Prosecutor. Feeling his case slipping away, he looked beseechingly at Bannon, who stood a dozen feet away, next to Altman. Bannon shrugged.

"Jesse, if this bothers you, why don't you just leave?" Bannon said. "After all, this is a private house and until something happens, as Belinda says, you don't have much say in the matter, do you?"

Defeat crumpled Gimball's face. Mumbling, he joined his wife and began gathering his things to leave, but then changed his mind. He barged back into the group. "All right. Let's see what the hell this is all about."

A mahogany table was cleared of the remaining hors d'oeuvres. Sampson sat at one end of it facing the audience, who were seated on chairs and a sofa. Voisin removed a small leather pouch from his pocket and withdrew half a dozen plastic tubes. He held up one of them for inspection. The needle inside gleamed and the guests exclaimed as they recognized what it was. Carelessly, Voisin picked up a small plate from a stack on an end table. He carried it to the bar and poured a trifle of Scotch into it. He returned with the plate, unpacked two needles, and dropped them into the Scotch.

"Simple sterilization, as a precaution. One of the beauties of needle therapy is that it can be performed successfully without all the trappings of Western medicine. Now, Mr. Trehune, if you please."

Sampson turned away from the audience, resting his head on a folded napkin which Voisin had prepared. He wished the table had some give to it. He also wished he wasn't in the same grubby sport shirt Abel had bought him. And those ugly shoes.

Looking up, he saw Voisin wave a needle with his usual magician's air. The doctor moved beyond Sampson's vision and the next thing Sampson knew, his left ear was being folded forward. Now comes the lecture, Sampson thought, remembering Voisin's penchant for talk. Waiting, he smelled the Scotch in the saucer near him. His mouth had never felt so dry. He tried to recall the passages from Voisin's book which described the miraculous cures of deaf children, to recall what the treatment should feel like, to recall, above all else, the sensation of sound. He began counting to himself, muscles tightening a little in anticipation of the needle.

Voisin released his ear and once more the doctor's face was visible. "So," he announced. "Mr. Trehune, the other side."

"It's over?" Sampson croaked.

"But of course. Now, the right side."

Instinctively, Sampson raised his hand and rubbed behind his left ear. Nothing. He listened, strained to receive whatever miracle might be forthcoming. Nothing.

Voisin tapped his shoulder. "The right side, please."

Sampson put his head back down on the napkin and closed his eyes. So important and he hadn't been aware of a thing. Didn't seem fair. Soon Voisin tapped him again, and he opened his eyes. The audience was on its feet. They moved close to peer into Sampson's face.

"Well?" demanded Abel.

Sampson just shook his head. He probably looked as he felt—confused and foolish.

"Rest a minute, Mr. Trehune. Perhaps a drink?" Sampson's heart leapt and he almost cried "God, yes," but then he realized that Voisin didn't mean Scotch.

Dr. Altman appeared with a glass of orange juice he had taken from the bar, and Sampson gulped it thirstily. I must be really dry, he thought. "More," he said, and was supplied with a second glass. Thirst satisfied, he waited and listened. Or did what he supposed was listening.

"It will take approximately a half-hour before we can determine if the procedure has been successful," Voisin said.

"Is there a place where Mr. Trehune could lie down and be comfortable?"

Lucky, Sampson thought, as he watched most of the group move toward the bar before he followed Mrs. Bannon to a bedroom on the second floor. At least Belinda had given him the Churchill victory sign. He thought the fingers of her other hand were probably crossed behind her back.

The light breeze that had been blowing earlier in the evening had picked up force. Sampson felt a surge of fresh air when he entered the guest room. The window curtains billowed and the door was nearly tugged out of his hand as he closed it after Mrs. Bannon. The queen-size bed beckoned. The spread had been removed, draped carefully over an armchair. Two large white pillows were plumped one on top of the other.

He tried to pace the room energetically, to ignore the invitation. He supposed he was once more experiencing that fatalistic ennui most patients feel when they finally, irrevocably, give themselves over to the god medicine.

God! Sampson tried to haul himself to a sitting position. Dimly he recalled deciding to sit on the edge of the bed—for just a minute, just one beautiful, restorative minute. When had he stretched out, accepted the invitation?

Well, maybe he would try sitting up later. Nothing wrong with taking a few minutes off. Vaguely he waved his heavy, limp left hand before his eyes. He couldn't focus to see the time. Besides, the hot light from the night-stand lamp irritated them. Proof that his eyes needed a rest. They were very tired. Leaden, dead tired.

Dead? I've been drugged, thought Sampson. This time he really tried to sit up, but he couldn't. He was pulled deeper into the soft, scented pillows. "Bother." His lips formed the word, then slackened.

When the door closed, he was conscious of a new sensation.

He had actually heard it slam. Heard it. Another sensation startled him. Outside the window, beyond the room, was another sound. He heard it. A train whistle? A dog yowling? Dear God, he had so much to learn. His arm was crooked beneath his head and, curious, he moved his watch closer to his ear.

No, it did not go ticktock, as he had read so often and had sworn he could remember from his childhood. The watch went . . . it went dinka dinka dinka. That was it: dinka-dinkadinkadinka. Well, that's all right. I don't really mind, he thought. Smiling, he turned on his back. He wanted to raise his arm and look at the dinka—

Dr. Richard Altman hovered over him like an avenging angel from the family Bible. He held a needle in his right hand, which was poised, ready to strike.

Sampson shifted his shoulders and grabbed Altman's wrist. Altman's left hand closed over Sampson's throat, squeezing fingers and seemingly the full weight of his body on Sampson's windpipe. Sampson twisted and struggled, finally breaking free, but the needle came perilously close, and he jerked his head away just in time. He felt the needle scratch his nose.

Sampson couldn't tell how long the struggle lasted. A few seconds, a minute, ten minutes. He seemed engaged in a bizarre wrestling match taking place in a tub of molasses. But he heard Altman's heavy breathing—not just felt it, not just smelled it, but heard it. He heard the muttered curses of the doctor as he knelt on Sampson's right arm, pinning him temporarily to the bed. He moved in with the acupuncture needle. Sampson heard a sound like . . . like "argghhh," and knew it came from within himself.

"Damn." He heard his own voice. "Damn." Idiotically, he repeated the word over and over, concentrating on the sound. He even smiled, listening to it: "Damn. Damn." He was delighted by the sound. He could hear. Happiness flooded him like sudden sunshine—until he realized he was about to die.

Slowly, painfully, he dislodged Altman and reached toward his pocket—toward rescue in the only form he had ever known. His fingers struggled to get inside the narrow pants pocket. He rolled over again, to avoid the jabbing needle. His fingers closed on the flat plastic case. He pressed the button and flung the case up toward Altman's face. Altman pushed it away and down, until the object rested on Sampson's temple. It was triggered.

The room exploded in a kaleidoscope of pain. Lights burned with such intensity that they merged into one searing sphere. The light itself opened and Sampson fell in.

Sampson opened his eyes.

"O.K.?" Abel signed.

Sampson nodded.

"Devil of a time. What a racket!" Abel picked up the small black box and waved it in front of Sampson. It was a pocket alarm. "We got him." Abel put the box down. "First time I ever saw someone petrified by sound."

Sound. Sampson dropped his gaze. His eyes happened to focus on his watch. Subconsciously he noted that an hour had passed since he had entered the room. Time later for that. What he wanted to think about now was sound.

Abel shook his shoulder. "What's the matter? Sure you're O.K.?"

Sampson smiled, felt his muscles flexing with laughter. "Sure," he signed. "You haven't forgotten why I'm—"

"My God! Can you hear?"

"No," said Sampson, reading Abel's words.

"I am sorry, my friend." This from Voisin, who had come to Abel's side.

"But I did," articulated Sampson. "I heard."

155

Voisin stared back at him, nodded. "Not impossible or even unusual. You know, sometimes hearing is restored briefly. Only for minutes. Then . . ." Voisin made the universal gesture of a bird flying from the hand.

"Saved my life," Sampson articulated again. "Door slammed. Woke me up."

"Drugged?" asked Abel.

Sampson nodded.

"That alarm of yours—extraordinarily loud. It was found right beside your head," Voisin said.

Sampson nodded again, recalling the pain. He had not been surprised when he awakened to his normal state, silence.

"Anyway," Abel talked excitedly, "we got him."

"Not him," Sampson announced. "Them!"

But no one was listening. He had lost his audience. They were transfixed, facing the door. They must have heard something. The next moment, they were bolting from the bedroom. Sampson followed woozily.

An incredible tableau stopped him just inside the library. Sprawled on the beige rug was Belinda Shaw. Leaning against the desk, a smoking revolver in his hand, was Morton Bannon, his wife by his side. Abel, Voisin, and two other guests stood motionless. A policeman, gun drawn, looked confused.

"What happened?" Sampson asked, and everybody started talking at once. Sampson kept his eyes on Abel, who bent over Shaw.

"A bump on the head," he said. "Nothing serious, from the looks of it."

Voisin darted across to the library desk, and for the first time Sampson noticed a pair of legs sticking out from behind it.

The policeman took the gun from Bannon, who seemed dazed and made no attempt to retain the weapon. "It happened so fast," he said.

"What happened?" demanded the policeman.

"After Abel and Voisin left," Bannon said, "Altman hit Miss Shaw with an ashtray, and started for me. I just had time to reach my desk and get that gun when he was on me. We struggled, and I fired. How is he?"

The policeman tucked Bannon's gun in his belt and, like everyone else, watched Abel and Voisin, who knelt over Altman.

"I doubt if he'll live. Seems to be internal hemorrhaging. Bullet's lodged close to his heart," said Abel, standing up.

Voisin, however, rushed past Sampson, out of the room, ignoring the apparent shouts of the policeman. Confusion seemed to grow by the second. He returned, three needles in his hand, and, to the policeman's astonishment, ripped off Altman's shirt and began to insert a needle in his neck.

"Hold it," the policeman said, menacing Voisin with his gun.

Startled, Voisin looked up.

"It's all right, Johnny," said Belinda Shaw, slowly sitting up. "Let him try."

"Yes, ma'am, if you say so." The policeman looked doubtful and more confused, but he lowered his gun.

Moments later, Voisin arose, triumphant. "He will live, at least until you can get him to the hospital and remove the bullet. If your doctors don't bungle that job, he should recover without incident."

Abel stooped over Altman, examined him carefully. "He just might," he said finally. "That's amazing, absolutely amazing."

Voisin smiled and gave a shrug, but obviously he was enjoying himself. "What I did was a simple procedure described in a treatise on first aid written nearly two thousand years ago. The only amazing thing is the arrogance of Western physicians who refuse . . ."

He's off again, thought Sampson, who moved unsteadily to Belinda Shaw. He almost fell over as he bent down to help her to her feet. They stood together for a moment, bracing each other.

"Mrs. Bannon, could I have a glass of water, please?" Shaw asked faintly.

"Why, of course. Poor dear, how thoughtless of me." She left for the kitchen.

Bannon moved closer to Altman. "This I have to see."

Shaw raised her hand to her forehead, which obviously still pained her. "Johnny," she said, "Johnny, I may pass out again, but keep Mr. Bannon here until the rest of the police and Lieutenant Hodges arrive. Don't let him near Dr. Altman. In fact, if Mr. Bannon moves at all, shoot him, Johnny."

Patrolman Johnny Jones looked incredulous, but he raised his pistol toward Bannon, who stopped in mid-stride as he rounded the desk. "I don't quite understand this, Mr. Bannon, but please stand over there, away from everyone." He looked as if he meant business, now that he had a definite order to carry out, and Bannon did as he was instructed.

"I don't understand this, either," Bannon said, glaring, "and I wish someone would explain."

Sampson said calmly, "No. You explain. For the record, of course."

Shaw seemed revived. "Yes, please do, Mr. Bannon, just for the record."

"This is nonsense. Some ridiculous macabre joke you're all playing, I suppose."

"No mistake," Shaw continued. "Harriet Stone—or Jennifer Reed, if you prefer—was picked up this afternoon at her apartment, thanks to Mr. Trehune. And with her statement, plus a basketful of evidence the New York authorities found there, you're quite finished, Mr. Bannon." As an afterthought, she added, "Read him his rights, Johnny. He's under arrest for murder and conspiracy, grand theft, fraud, and a few other charges."

Bannon made an effort to control his features, but Sampson could read defeat beginning to etch its way into them. And as his jaw finally slackened and his eyes dulled, Sampson imagined he could see the collapse of the Bannon empire happening there. Or what was left of it.

FOURTEEN

Henri Voisin was visibly nervous as he paced the length of the Shaw living room, moving from the stone fireplace to the foot of the stairs, turning and retracing his steps. It was particularly distracting to the other three in the room. Two of them, Abel and Shaw, did not understand his nervousness. The third, Sampson Trehune, understood and was disturbed for that very reason. He had a choice to make, a choice he didn't relish, because no matter what he chose, it would not be wholly right.

Voisin stopped his pacing and stared at the Early American clock which occupied a prominent place on Belinda Shaw's living-room wall. Both Abel and Shaw joined him in staring at the clock. The hands were together, pointing straight up. Midnight. The damn thing is probably striking, Sampson thought. What does a clock striking sound like? He closed his eyes and tried to remember a time in his childhood when he had heard a clock strike. It was nearly impossible, like trying to recall the exact savor of penny candy chewed greedily on a long-ago Saturday afternoon. He gave up trying. He would never hear again.

When Sampson opened his eyes, Voisin had resumed pacing. Probably, Sampson thought, Abel and Shaw assumed his behavior was just eccentricity. After Altman had been rushed to his own clinic and Bannon had been jailed in a building he had personally contributed a large sum to construct, everyone relaxed. Except Voisin.

"And now, what of me?" Voisin asked, coming to a second halt. Shaw reminded him that the only charge he had to worry about was contempt of court. The trial had been postponed for another week, but she could—and would—persuade the state not to prosecute. In fact, she had already started the paper work to that end.

"Then I am free?" Voisin asked. "And my passport?"

"Here," she said, handing Voisin the stiff dark blue booklet with its gold Embassy seal which she took from her purse. "I'm sticking my neck out but . . . you deserve it."

"Is there an airport?" He had lost an entire week, he explained, and was soon due in China, where he and others would undertake much-needed research to determine whether acupuncture points existed on internal organs.

"But surely just an extra day or two?" Abel suggested.

"No, I must leave now. Time is so precious." Checking a schedule, Belinda Shaw discovered an early morning flight from Tweed Airport in New Haven which would return Voisin to New York.

"Is this New Haven near?"

"Not too far. And since you insist upon leaving, the least we can do is provide you with a ride to the airport. One of Lieutenant Hodges's men will drive you." Reasonable, Sampson thought. Every member of the Hastings police force had been on duty this evening, handling the normal Saturday night

160

chores, as well as forming a group to raid the Bannon plant. Now they were probably standing around trying to look busy.

"I still don't understand," Abel said. "Dr. Altman actually murdered Harrison Wolberg? With the needles? And there was no trace, nothing which could be found in the autopsy?"

Voisin launched an explanation that was terse, almost hasty, a contrast to his usual showmanship. "You are a neurologist, as well as a psychiatrist, Dr. Abel?" he said, approaching him. "So, open your jacket." Voisin quickly bent over the doctor and touched the area around his heart. "Here, just above and to the right of your heart." Voisin pushed slightly and the doctor winced. "There, at that precise point, a nerve which leads from the heart to the brain approaches the surface of the skin. If a needle pierced that point, perhaps just once, perhaps as many as three times, can you imagine what would happen?"

Abel shrugged at the apparently silly question, and thought for a moment. "Pain in the chest perhaps, and maybe a headache? If the flow of blood, say, were disturbed . . ."

Voisin silenced the doctor with a contemptuous wave of his hand. "Bah! After such a puncture, the patient would exhibit every symptom of madness. He would indeed be mad! A perfectly normal human being would suddenly be placed in a strait jacket and locked up. You would try drugs, tranquilizers, or perhaps a lengthy therapy where you strove to discover a clue to his madness in his childhood. His relations with his mother, for example. When, all the time, a simple needle, the same which caused the madness, can cure it."

Voisin warmed to his subject, his nervousness forgotten. At least it's better than his pacing, thought Sampson. "Now, there are several points—the points of death, as they are called. Many studies—most, in fact—never mention them. They are points which must never be pierced. This is what your Dr.

161

Altman did when he went in to examine Harrison Wolberg last Sunday night. He pierced a point on the cheek, directly below the eye, which caused Wolberg's death almost instantly. It looked like a heart attack, according to Western medical examination. But when I read Wolberg's pulses after his death, I knew it couldn't have been heart stoppage. The pulses were all wrong for that. It was not until later, thanks to Mr. Trehune's curiosity and his description of Claire Fletcher's face, that everything became clear."

Abel said, "But why was Altman frightened enough of Harrison Wolberg to actually murder him?" With the arrest of Altman, and Bannon, Abel had grown belligerently aware that things had happened, were happening, which he simply did not understand.

"Altman was not frightened of him, but Bannon sure as hell was." Sampson's hands were speaking to Abel, patiently. "Bannon was sure that Wolberg had discovered his deceptions regarding the financial structure of Bannon Electronics. Wolberg had to be stopped, quickly, quietly, or Bannon was finished. So he pressured Altman into murdering him."

Abel cut him off. "But why? How?"

"Are you two talking about Dr. Altman?" Shaw broke in. Abel nodded, and she continued, "Again, thanks to Sampson, a link between the two was discovered." Abel raised his eyebrows at the familiar use of his friend's first name. "Altman and Bannon were receiving thousands of dollars each year in kickbacks from Bannon's medical supply firm. The company sold an inferior line of disposable medical products but, thanks to Altman, had an exclusive contract with the clinic—as well as several other hospitals and clinics which Bannon, through Altman, succeeded in signing up. Bannon threatened exposure unless Altman cooperated in the extortion. He could do it, too, without implicating himself. Bannon could exert further

162

pressure on Altman because he knew that the clinic was performing abortions. In fact, I think that a former employee of Bannon's, who became his mistress, was one of Altman's patients and aborted Bannon's child in the clinic."

Abel was plainly unsatisfied. "So?"

Sampson's fingers flicked the answers. "Obvious. Opportunity, ability, and motivation. Who had them? In the death of Harrison Wolberg, after eliminating the other physicians present, it had to be Altman—or you. That of course explains the nineteenth needle. In case something did go wrong, in case he was searched, in case the police did not buy the story of a natural death, what better place to hide the murder weapon, a needle, than among a dozen and a half other needles? Nurse Harmon either saw Altman drop in the extra needle or guessed his part in the murder. Anyway, she had a passion for Altman. Now she was sure she would become Mrs. Altman and not just another nurse with afterhour duties. She was confident, and she let Altman know it."

Shaw was watching Sampson eagerly, but with a trace of misgiving. Obviously she didn't like being left out. Sampson looked at her, then nodded toward Abel and said slowly, "Claire Fletcher. Tell him." As Shaw began, Sampson felt Henri Voisin staring at him. Sampson had stuck his foot squarely in his mouth. He had brought up the one subject he most wanted to avoid.

"Again, it was mostly Sampson's idea. As long as we looked for just one person, Henri Voisin seemed headed straight for the electric chair. If we assumed, as both Lieutenant Hodges and I did, that the deaths of Harrison Wolberg and Claire Fletcher were related, then Voisin seemed the only person with the opportunity and the ability to carry out the murders. What puzzled us was the apparent lack of any motive." She paused to smile in the direction of Voisin, and Sampson again

163

noted the tension in the acupuncturist's expression. He smiled, but beneath his smile Sampson could discern strained, taut muscles.

Heedless of the tension building up around her, Shaw continued, addressing Voisin. "But, thanks to Sampson, I was convinced of your innocence, and last evening when you detailed how Wolberg's death could have resulted from just a needle—well, that narrowed the field considerably. Then, with Fletcher murdered in an attempt to use the same method, we were put on the right track. We started looking for two murderers, not just one. After all, as Sampson pointed out, if someone could kill Wolberg with such terrifying efficiency, that same person would not have botched the job on poor Claire Fletcher."

"But how could Bannon—"

Sampson's hands broke into the conversation again. "You and your damned chess game. When you're stuck at the board, your sense of time becomes distorted. With Altman to distract you, could you be sure exactly how long Bannon was absent from the room? Or his house, for that matter? Remember, it's only a five-minute drive to the Blue Coat from Bannon's home. He had called Fletcher several times; she kept waiting for him, getting drunker.

"He finally arrives, Fletcher opens the side door near the restaurant for him. The night clerk doesn't see him. He accompanies her up to her room, using the rear stairway. Inside her room, he knocks her out, and starts to needle her face. He realizes it's impossible, and smothers her when she starts to regain consciousness. Another quick trip to the first floor, for some kerosene, and he hopes the fire will destroy his handiwork. It turned out better than he hoped; the authorities blamed Voisin for both the fire and Fletcher's death."

Abel thought for a minute, and said, "Yes, I suppose Bannon could have been gone longer than I thought. But still—"

"At most, the whole scheme required half an hour. Bannon's suit undoubtedly smelled of smoke and kerosene, but he could pass it off to his wife as just some difficulty in starting the car. It's doubtful that she would be aware of the difference between gasoline and kerosene smells, between exhaust smoke and any other kind. But he couldn't take a chance with you, or Harmon.

"So he shunts you both off on Altman, and he and his wife drive off. By the time you arrive, he's already rushed into the burning hotel and has a perfect cover for the appearance and odor of his clothes."

"Then Nurse Harmon wasn't in on the plan?"

Shaw, pleased to know what was being discussed, answered, "No, I'm sure she wasn't. She knew enough about last Sunday to keep Altman friendly, but she was completely ignorant of Bannon's involvement. It would be extremely difficult, under the circumstances, to get a conviction on conspiracy charges, and I doubt if the state will even try. It'll be a long time before she works as a nurse, though. I'll see to that."

Excitedly, Sampson waved for Abel's attention. "She would have her patients on pins and needles." Abel must have groaned, for both Shaw and Voisin looked from him to Sampson and back again, worried. Finally, the doctor translated Sampson's tooth-grinding joke, which was greeted with appropriate signs of disgust by all. Bother, Sampson thought.

Abel continued trying to piece together the web of motives which had led to Fletcher's death. "So Bannon discovered that Fletcher was on to him, that she was pursuing the same path Wolberg had discovered. Therefore, she had to be killed."

Again Sampson felt the searching, nervous gaze of Henri Voisin. Well, it's now or never, Sampson thought. On the previous evening—Friday—he, Voisin, and Belinda Shaw had sat in this same room. She had listened while he and the acupuncturist recounted both the facts and the conclusions to

165

which they inescapably led. No mention had been made on Friday night of the real nature of Claire Fletcher's investigations or of the story which Voisin had spun for Sampson earlier that day in the Hastings jail.

Sampson had no wish to deceive Abel and Shaw. Nor did he wish to withhold evidence. Voisin's story, embellished or straight, had no substantive bearing on the death of either Wolberg or Fletcher. Was it really evidence? A line from Homer flitted through his mind, about retribution coming to an end someday. In addition, with Voisin discredited, the whole future of acupuncture in the West might also suffer. Too often, he knew, Hearers used any pretext to dismiss an alien idea or practice. He jerked himself out of such thoughts to find all three staring at him.

"I said that Fletcher must have discovered what Wolberg found out," Abel repeated, more of a question than a statement.

Sampson answered, in his best voice, "Yes, Claire Fletcher was simply retracing the same steps as Wolberg, and Bannon decided she had to be removed." Voisin visibly relaxed, and he nodded briefly at Sampson when he caught his eye. "All her notes destroyed in fire. Pity. Mine, too. That's why we had to prod Altman into doing something desperate at Bannon's party. We had absolutely no proof against him that would stand up in court."

"But how could you know he would act?" Abel asked.

"Oh, we weren't at all sure," Belinda Shaw replied. "But it was worth a chance." She looked at Sampson rather sadly, and he shook his head. Yes, it was probably worth it. And it had been his idea. "You see, at the party, I cornered Altman and in the presence of Gimball I let drop that Sampson and Voisin thought Wolberg was murdered and that they had requested me to get an exhumation order for the body, which would have been all but impossible, given the jurisdictions in-

166

volved. But Altman panicked, and when he saw his chance, he decided to get rid of both Sampson and Voisin at the same time. He drugged the orange juice which Sampson took after the acupuncture treatment, so that it would be easy to dispose of him the same way he had disposed of Wolberg. With Sampson's death immediately following the needle treatment, just like Wolberg's and apparently from the same cause—well, Voisin would be discredited, to say the least, and his theories about mysterious murders would be viewed as so much ridiculous subterfuge. It was a neat idea, and Altman came much too close to carrying it out. As I understand it, the pulses last for just a short time after death, and the only person available who could read them was you, Henri, and who would have believed you? By the time someone else had been brought in, even another acupuncturist, the pulses would have ceased, naturally. And there would be no evidence whatsoever."

Yes, much too close, Sampson thought ruefully. He'd been an idiot, so busy thinking about a needle attempt that he'd ignored the orange juice. And there was the thought of hearing. He looked at the three, and they were smiling. Since their mouths were open, they were probably laughing. What did laughter sound like? He had read scores of poetic descriptions of silver, golden, hollow, menacing laughter. But he could never really know, never experience just how someone like Belinda sounded when she was happy.

Voisin, standing near Sampson, reached down and with two fingers pushed the corners of Sampson's mouth into an answering smile. Audacious, but effective. Sampson smiled naturally in return. "Just thinking," he said lamely in explanation.

"Don't!" the Frenchman ordered. "It is just like when I first saw you. You are feeling sorry for yourself. That is a great mistake, my friend. A great mistake. We are living on the threshold of a great era. The future is bright. Even for you. You know, it is quite common for deaf persons to experience a temporary recovery of hearing after the first needle treatment. But this gain is frequently short-lived. Hearing becomes permanent only after continued treatment—three months, six months, perhaps more. Tonight you heard. Granted, that alarm may have damaged your inner ear. Future treatment may be more difficult, if not impossible. But only perhaps. Wait for a few months, then try the needles again. In the meantime . . ." he finished the sentence with a smile and a shrug which seemed to be aimed toward Belinda Shaw.

As they looked at her, Belinda suddenly arose and started to leave the room. Halfway into the hall she stopped and, for Sampson's benefit, pointed at the door chimes on the wall. She left the room and returned with the same pudgy sergeant whom Sampson had met on Friday afternoon.

Poor Henri, Sampson thought. Stuck with the sergeant's transistor radio and the worst of American pop music. But he should have known better. After being introduced, Voisin studied the officer and said, "But, Sergeant—my God, you are fat. You, an officer of the law, to be so gross, it is criminal."

Bewilderment changed to anger on the sergeant's face, and Sampson noticed that his hands were unconsciously forming fists. "A man's gotta eat," said the fat, sullen face.

"But, my dear sir, hunger is simply a function of the nerve endings in the stomach. When the stomach is distended, as I am afraid yours is, then more of the nerve endings are exposed. But an acupuncturist can curb your so-called hunger, can cut off those sensations from your stomach nerves, and your stomach will shrink accordingly." The sergeant, still skeptical, looked from the doctor to his spreading paunch and back again. "Yeah?" he finally said.

"Most assuredly. Why, over the past several years my colleague Dr. Mauries, of France, has successfully employed needle therapy on dozens of obese patients. The results are

168

most encouraging. Why . . ." Belinda escorted them to the door.

Abel, looking slightly uncomfortable, crossed his legs and gazed around, searching. "The john's upstairs, down the hall, second door on the right," Sampson signed and smiled.

Abel regarded his friend with amusement. "So this is where you spent Friday night. At least you could have told me."

Sampson waved away his criticism. "Henri and I were here discussing Wolberg's death with Belinda."

"But Dr. Voisin returned to the Hastings jail, whereas you did not."

"For his own safety. I didn't need protection."

"I wasn't thinking about you."

"Slept right here," Sampson said, patting the couch cushion. "Also, there was a maid."

Abel remained unconvinced, marched up the stairs, and disappeared.

About to enter the living room, Belinda retraced her steps quickly. She reappeared with Henri Voisin. "He wants to give you something," she said. Noticing the doctor's nervousness, she added, "Excuse me a minute, I'm going to change into something more comfortable." She, too, climbed the stairs, Sampson following her ankles until they vanished. He turned to Voisin, puzzled.

Henri Voisin held out a copy of his book, the same copy which Sampson had brought to the Hastings jail Friday. Voisin opened the book to the flyleaf, and once again Sampson saw his sketch of Claire Fletcher's face, with the needle marks just beneath her eyes.

Voisin scribbled a few words beneath the woman's face, and, apparently, added a signature. He closed the volume and handed it to Sampson, who forced himself not to open it immediately and read the name. Voisin nodded his thanks as Sampson placed the book on a table. When Sampson got up, the acupuncturist embraced him and said, "Good-bye, my friend. Good luck."

And he was gone, the Don Quixote of acupuncture. Good luck to you, Sampson added silently, watching for a moment as the police car sped into the night. Have they got the siren going? he wondered as he closed the door.

Seating himself on Belinda's comfortable couch, Sampson was suddenly aware of a chill in the air. He shivered involuntarily. The October night had turned quite cold; he decided the old rambling Shaw house, two floors, fourteen rooms, must be a problem to heat. He had to admire Belinda's stubbornness in hanging on to it. She, like Sampson, was the last of her family. The last Shaw in Hastings, since her parents had both been killed in a car accident, she had told him, nearly five years before. Being the last of a line, Sampson said to himself, brought special problems. He shivered again, and felt a twinge in his left shoulder. His stomach, where he skinned himself scrambling from his hotel window, was painful. His shoes hurt, too, and he thought fleetingly of removing them.

If the wall clock was correct, he and Abel had over an hour to kill before they left to catch the train to New York. An erratic milk train, it was usually at least an hour late, but you couldn't be sure.

He watched Abel and Belinda descend the stairs together, she having changed into a colorful paisley hostess gown. It suits her, Sampson noted: she's a rainbow. He tingled when he felt the silky material brush his hand as she sat down next to him.

"Are you going to sit there grinning to yourself all night," Abel said, interrupting his thoughts. "There are some questions!"

"Sore throat," Sampson signed. "I can't talk much. A drink would help."

170

With a show of pomp and patience, Abel turned and said, "Miss Shaw, Mr. Trehune would like a drink. For medicinal reasons, I'm sure."

"Of course. Forgive me, but I gave the maid the weekend off and I don't really entertain enough to be a good hostess." She started to rise, but Sampson reached up and held her arm lightly a moment. He leaned forward so the doctor could see his hands, and signed, "There's only Scotch. The bottle is in the cupboard beneath the kitchen sink. There are glasses in the cabinet above. The ice is in the refrigerator. Don't forget some water." Abel glared and huffed his way into the kitchen.

"So Frizzy Hair's off for the weekend?" he asked as soon as Abel left the room.

"Yes," Shaw said, smiling at him. "Her brother's children were coming down with something. She wanted to visit them. I didn't have anything planned, so I sent her on her way. It will give me a chance to putter around a bit, and she does make me nervous at times. She's a dear, really, but she's always underfoot."

Sampson agreed, and was about to add a comment or two about the sweet old dear when Abel returned, carrying a tray. "My, you were quick," Sampson signed peevishly.

"I am also curious and I feel I am entitled to some sort of explanation." The wounded Abel quickly filled three glasses with ice and Scotch, topping each with a splash of water. A rite of initiation, his manner said.

"You talk, I'll sign," Sampson said, drinking deeply and relaxing. He actually felt comfortable for the first time in over a week, in spite of his aches and pains. He could sympathize with Abel, of course. He had not confided in his friend, nor told him about his excursions to Wolberg's apartment and the brokerage firm or of his talk with Voisin on Friday. Hence, from Abel's point of view, the pronouncements and conclu-

171

sions which issued from Sampson and Belinda were oracular. Smug and self-satisfied, Sampson did nothing to dispel this notion. His hands began to tell a story.

"He says he was suspicious from the very beginning," Abel spoke, adding, "but I would discount that. He was undoubtedly curious, nothing more." Now it was Sampson's turn to glare. Before he could proceed further, however, both Abel and Belinda turned their heads toward the hall, Belinda quickly rising. Must be the damned door again. Who now?

Jesse Gimball entered, County Prosecutor extraordinary. Shaw followed him, alternately amused and angry. Gimball's face was a study. Words tumbled from his mouth incoherently as far as Sampson could see. He was literally sputtering. His features were lined in anger, and the deep red of his cheeks and temples was the product of rage. Puce, Sampson thought. That's Gimball's color: puce.

Gimball had left the Bannon home almost immediately after Sampson had been treated by Voisin. His long-suffering wife had led him, rather the worse for drink, from an argument with Voisin which threatened to become ugly. Now he looked at Sampson with ill-concealed distaste, and demanded of the three of them, "Where is he? That crazy needle doctor or whatever he calls himself. Where is he?"

"Sorry, Jesse, but you just missed him by about twenty minutes," Belinda said.

"Well, damn it, get him back here. Or, better still, get him down to the station. Pronto! There are questions, by God, and he better have some answers."

Without being asked, Gimball reached for the bottle and looked around for a glass. Since Shaw was obviously busy, Abel got him one and added ice.

"That won't really be necessary," Shaw said as Gimball took a swallow and sputtered once more, choking.

"Not necessary! Do you know who just called and got me

out of bed? Do you? Haslip, that's who. Morton Bannon's personal lawyer. Do you know that they've got Morton Bannon, *the* Morton Bannon, in the hoosegow at this very minute? And that fool Hodges wouldn't release him, not on his own recognizance nor even on bail. Why, I never heard of such a thing."

"Surely, Counselor, you know that bail is routinely denied in a capital crime."

"Capital crime! Don't tell me you believe Hodges? Why, that's silly. Morton Bannon? A capital crime?"

"Of course I agree with Lieutenant Hodges. In fact, most of what he did this evening was by my order—or, more accurately, my suggestion, since he is a municipal official and I represent the county."

"You. You! And I suppose you put Hodges up to breaking into Bannon's plant? You know Bannon Electronics is outside the city limits of Hastings. He had no right—"

Shaw wearily broke into his near-hysterical speech. "Don't quibble over jurisdiction. Lieutenant Hodges was accompanied by an officer from the staff of the County Prosecutor's office, and was armed with a search warrant, duly authorizing him to enter and examine the said premises and to impound any evidence he might find there."

"What evidence?"

"The books of Bannon Electronics, for a start. They are now under lock and key in my office. While you and I were enjoying ourselves last evening, Lieutenant Hodges was in the process of locking up Bannon's books until an independent state auditor can have a look at them. Similar moves were carried out in New York and Philadelphia. The books of New England Med-Art, Incorporated, and Electronetics are also in custody, and both states have agreed to cooperate with our auditors to determine precisely the extent of Bannon's theft."

173

She paused and emptied her glass, and Sampson was on his feet, quickly refilling it. He smiled at her as he handed her the glass, their hands touching briefly. "If our suspicions are correct, I'm sure that the Securities and Exchange Commission will want to get into the act," she said. "But since a capital crime is involved and was committed in Connecticut, we are of course claiming prior jurisdiction, and holding him for prosecution."

"Suspicions? You mean you locked up Morton Bannon on just suspicions? Belinda Shaw, you're making an ass of yourself!"

Abel sat quietly, trying to follow the exchange between the two officials and its implications. Sampson also sat quietly, thoroughly enjoying the sight of Belinda in action. She's smooth, he thought, very smooth.

"There are more than just suspicions, Jesse. For a beginning, Morton Bannon is being held for murder in the first degree—that's premeditated, Counselor. He is an accessory to a second murder, also first degree. He is being charged with conspiracy in the case of the first murder. And with grand theft, fraud, and embezzlement. Of course, that's just the beginning. I have no doubt we will discover that Mr. Bannon had other shortcomings as well."

Gimball was about to reply, but she turned and walked from the room, catching Sampson's eye as she did so, and mimed talking into a telephone. Gimball glared at both men, said nothing, but filled his glass again.

After an absence of several minutes, Shaw appeared in the doorway and paused until all eyes were upon her. She turned her head toward Sampson so he would be sure of seeing what she said.

"That was Lieutenant Hodges, from the Altman Clinic. Dr. Richard Altman will live, thanks to the quick work of Henri Voisin. He should be able to stand trial within a month. He

174

was conscious long enough to make a brief statement. It was Morton Bannon who struck me, and then shot Altman. It was also Morton Bannon who killed Claire Fletcher last Thursday and touched off the fire to cover his tracks. We can add arson to the list of charges against him." She paused, hesitating. "Mrs. Bannon was just brought into the emergency room. She slashed her wrists in a suicide attempt, and would have succeeded if a servant hadn't decided to do a bit of cleaning after the party instead of waiting until tomorrow morning. She might pull through, but the doctors can't say for sure."

"Oh, my God," said Gimball, and fell heavily into a chair. "This just can't be true."

"I'm afraid it is, Jesse. Morton Bannon will be joining some pretty illustrious company. You remember the case of Tony de Angelis and his Allied Crude Vegetable Oil Refining Company. A very fancy name. He succeeded in milking some of the most prestigious Wall Street firms of nearly two hundred million dollars by the simple expedient of fake warehouse receipts which stated that his tanks down at Bayonne, New Jersey, contained salad oil. They were actually filled with water. And a Texas millionaire named Billie Sol Estes? He secured fantastic loans by offering tanks of liquid fertilizer as collateral. The tanks were actually empty. It happens, Counselor, even in Hastings, Connecticut."

Gimball just sat, staring blankly and nodding his head. "Poor Constance Bannon. And her father, Senator Ellis. This will just about kill the poor old man."

"Poor Claire Fletcher," Sampson blurted. "And Harry Wolberg."

Gimball looked at him dubiously, then turned to Shaw. "You are sure? No possible mistake? Altman isn't just trying to save his own skin?"

She shook her head. "There's more than just Altman's statement. Saturday afternoon, acting on information supplied by my office, New York City police apprehended one Jennifer Reed, at the same time seizing several bankbooks found in her apartment. Eighteen in all, at different New York banks. These books alone—and there are undoubtedly more—indicated deposits of close to a million dollars. Cash. Two accounts were in her name, the rest were in the name of Morton Bannon." She paused to let this information sink in.

"She had no idea what was happening, not actually. But she must have decided that the whole scheme was falling apart. She waived extradition proceedings, and is being returned to Hastings tomorrow. Do you remember an attractive young woman named Harriet Stone? Worked as a private secretary for Morton Bannon for several years, left Hastings about two years ago? Harriet Stone and Jennifer Reed are the same person."

Gimball placed his drink, half finished, on an end table, and once more just shook his head. Belinda continued, "In her preliminary statement to the New York police, she has confessed but minimized her role. Naturally, she is looking for a plea-bargaining situation. She implicates Morton Bannon in a scheme to bleed his companies of all possible cash. The two of them would skip to Brazil with the proceeds and live happily ever after. She was suspicious of Bannon's intentions toward Wolberg, but vehemently denies complicity in his death or in the death of Claire Fletcher. The evidence in hand, plus the statements of Altman and Stone, however, pretty well tie up the case."

"But what did he hope to gain?"

"Millions," Sampson interjected.

"Perhaps Mr. Trehune had better explain," Shaw said, "since it was really his information which led us to Bannon."

Sampson nodded and indicated to Abel that he should interpret. "Mr. Trehune wishes me to speak for him," Abel

176

said, and began giving sound to Sampson's quick-moving hands: "Bannon apparently started withdrawing large amounts of capital from his corporations over two years ago. He needed extra money to support Harriet Stone in New York. Then he hit upon the plan of taking everything he could lay his hands on and simply leaving the country with her. But his father-in-law, Senator Ellis, secured a lucrative government contract for Bannon Electronics, a contract which promised to put new life into the company. It was simply too good an opportunity to miss, because the contract also meant that Bannon could now raise a great deal more money. He returned the capital he had withdrawn, paid off the loans he had taken out for which he had offered his stock as collateral, and waited. Harrison Wolberg was a gift from heaven.

"Bannon knew Wolberg from college—a studious, spectacled, introverted person, scrupulous, unimaginative, and always just a bit out of it. As a partner in a brokerage house with an unquestioned reputation, Wolberg was perfect. Bannon approached him with the promise of a new government contract and a story about going public to raise needed capital. To Wolberg, the proposition seemed sound. The company was in a reasonably good financial position, and in a turnabout situation. Wolberg agreed without too much hesitation to have his firm underwrite the new issue.

"The value of the shares which Bannon and his wife held, plus the newly issued stock he had earmarked for corporate officers—namely, him and his wife—increased tremendously. From a corporation which had to depend upon subsidiaries to even stave off bankruptcy, Bannon Electronics now emerged as a company on the way up. Bannon could use his stock as leverage for loans of nearly ten times the value of his previous borrowings.

"But he wanted still more," Sampson signed, "and that's where Wolberg became suspicious. By using his position at the Electronetics subsidiary, Bannon started an ingenious exchange of shipments from the subsidiary to the parent company. The shipments were all worthless electrical components, but the invoices attached to them claimed they were needed parts for the new items to be manufactured under the impending government contract. Since Bannon claimed that it was classified, no one gave a thought to the shipments. Even the men still employed at Bannon were completely in the dark. So Morton Bannon could point to a warehouse filled with high-priced electrical components and raise still more money."

Gimball interrupted, "But surely someone, at some time, would have become suspicious. After all, when a company sells stock to the public—"

Sampson waved him silent. "As long as Bannon himself was in a key position to cook the books of both companies, there was literally nothing to discover. As far as the reports of the public accountants were concerned, they were accurate, and quite aboveboard, as long as the inventories and the whereabouts of blocks of company stock were accepted at face value. And since different accounting firms handled the books of the two companies, there was little possibility of cross-checking. Neither would suspect Bannon of deliberately sabotaging a much needed offering of public stock, an offering which would put his plant back on its feet again."

"But what happened to Harrison Wolberg?" Abel asked.

"Harriet Stone, alias Jennifer Reed, happened to poor Harry. To insure that Wolberg never got too interested in the Hastings plant, Bannon introduced him to Stone. She was to keep him busy and interested, which apparently she did. At least busy enough to stop his visits to you for therapy. He fell for her, hard. Not surprising, since she was undoubtedly the most beautiful girl who had ever even said hello to him. But somehow he became suspicious, and started checking Bannon Electronics' Hastings operation personally, and Morton Bannon decided he had to be removed. Then, when Claire Fletcher began investigating the death of Harrison Wolberg, Bannon assumed that she had also tumbled to his little scheme, and he disposed of her."

Gimball nodded his head and stood up. "I still don't understand this completely, but I assume you do, Belinda. I'll just take a quick run down to the station to see Haslip and keep him off your neck for a while." He started to leave, then paused. "If anything else happens, keep me informed. Please?" He looked pathetic, Sampson decided, puce and pathetic.

Shaw left the room with Gimball and was gone for a couple of minutes. Abel looked at Sampson and began to ask a question just as she returned. She swirled about the room, obviously enjoying herself. She poured the remains of the Scotch into their glasses, added ice, and emptied the ashtrays. As she was about to sit down, she glanced at the clock, and mimed talking into a telephone.

Damn. She was right of course, Sampson thought. He and Abel had only twenty minutes to reach the train station, on the off chance that the train would establish a record and be on time. She was telephoning for a cab to take them to the station. She had volunteered earlier to drive, but that had been vetoed by Sampson.

"You've had a busy day, and besides you're not dressed for it," he had relayed through Abel. She hadn't protested.

As soon as she left the room, Sampson's hands moved quickly. "Don't ask," he admonished, but could tell from the expression on Abel's face that he was going to have to explain at least in part. "Who else could it have been?" His hands pleaded. "Altman had scheduled Harrison Wolberg for treatment. The situation was tailor-made for disposing of him. And it wasn't probable that any other doctor present even knew that Wolberg was to be there. Remember, all they had were those abbreviated medical histories—no name, even. I saw mine; it identified me only as 'Male, Caucasian, Age 44, deaf since childhood.' Typical clinical information, medical history and brief work-up sheet, but nothing personal. I had to be introduced to every doctor present. I assume that Wolberg had to also. Who knew he was going to be there? You, Altman, myself."

"But how did you discover Jennifer Reed or Harriet Stone, or whatever her real name is?"

"Harriet Stone. She just picked Jennifer Reed at random when she began a bit of modeling in New York. But it's not so important how I discovered her. The real question is how Harrison Wolberg suddenly figured a link between his dazzling new mistress and Morton Bannon."

Patiently, Abel waited. When no answer was forthcoming, he leaned forward and slowly spelled, "W-e-l-l?"

In response, Sampson slowly spelled out a series of numbers, "60-12-211."

"S-o?"

"Bank number. Practically every bank in the country is now processing checks by computer, and each bank has been assigned an identification number. Look at a check sometime. The number is usually in the upper right-hand corner of every check drawn on an account in that particular bank. It is also on the deposit slip when a check from that bank is deposited in an account in another bank. Wolberg discovered a deposit slip for Jennifer Reed's account in her New York bank that made him suspicious."

Sampson spread a napkin on the end table and wrote on it in pencil, "60-12/211."

"The number 211 indicates the area or state in which the bank is located. In this instance, Connecticut, a number which Wolberg was quite familiar with, since Bannon's checks also had that number. When Stone stated that she received the check for modeling with a New York agency, Wolberg became immediately suspicious. He probably recalled that it was Bannon who had introduced him to Harriet. He spent all of his last week in Hastings, even standing Stone up for a theater date they had Wednesday night. Undoubtedly she called Bannon, who was probably already aware of Wolberg's snooping. He may not have been imaginative, but Wolberg was competent and thorough. He was also quite honest, so Bannon would have had no luck in trying to buy him. There was only one answer, and Altman was forced to kill Wolberg."

Belinda had returned and now sat, fascinated, watching the two men signing. "That's true," said Abel, speaking now in deference to her presence, "and I probably would have guessed that, but what about—"

"Can't explain everything," Sampson said, as grumpily as he could, and closed his eyes. He pictured Eeyore, the donkey, sitting in the river. "Eeyore, what are you doing there?" said Rabbit. "I'll give you three guesses, Rabbit." "Digging holes in the ground?" "Wrong." "Leaping from branch to branch of a young oak tree?" "Wrong." "Waiting for somebody to help you out of the river?" "Right. Give Rabbit time, and he'll always get the answer."

When he opened his eyes, Belinda was standing by a window, peering out into the night. She turned back to him and said, "Your cab's here."

While Abel shook Belinda's hand, Sampson got up slowly, took two steps, and seated himself again, clutching the arm of the sofa. "What is it?" Belinda asked.

"Undoubtedly Ménière's disease," Abel said dryly. "Quite common among deaf persons who have had some damage to the inner ear. Temporary dizziness, a touch of vertigo— nothing at all serious. Breathe deeply a few times, Sampson. You'll live. Come on, we'd better hurry."

181

Sampson rose unsteadily and accompanied Abel to the door. "Don't think I can make it," he squeaked.

"Please stay, there's plenty of room," said Belinda. "You're obviously in no condition to travel." Sampson nodded gratefully.

On the porch, shuffling his feet, was the toothless one, with the pink-and-black Chevrolet parked at the curb, its lights on and doors open. "Better hurry. She might be on time tonight. You never know."

Shaw was holding Sampson's arm. "You're going to stay," she said, and waved the driver back to the waiting car.

Standing beneath the porch light, Abel's fingers worked rapidly, both signing and spelling: "You're just a d-i-r-t-y-o-l—" Sampson closed the door.

A minute later, he was seated on Belinda's couch, a pillow plumped up behind his head and a blanket thrown over his knees. He had taken his shoes off. She seemed quite happy as she glided about, picking up the glasses. Suddenly she stopped and frowned. "The door," she said, her hands occupied with glasses.

"Let me," Sampson volunteered, and brushed aside her protests.

There he stood: green corduroy jacket, camera, and acne. His mouth was flapping furiously. Sampson waited, counted to thirty, then said, "We don't want any." And slammed the door.

"Who was it?" Belinda asked as she returned from the kitchen.

"Nobody."

"But the door chimes are still ringing," she said and moved toward the door.

"Ignore them. Pretend you are deaf."

"But I can't do that," she said and stopped. "It's the telephone." When she disappeared around the hall corner, Sampson pried up the plastic cover which hid the mechanism of the door chimes. He studied the wires for a moment, and then yanked one loose. The metal bar which moved to sound the chimes was still. He replaced the cover and turned to face Belinda, who was grinning.

"It's for you. A Mr. Heppish, or at least I think that's how you pronounce it. There's a terrible racket in the background. Sounds like the dog pound. Anyway, he wants to know when you'll be coming home. What shall I tell him?"

"Popcorn," replied Sampson. "Give him plenty of popcorn."

Bewildered, Belinda, followed by Sampson, returned to the telephone and repeated Sampson's cryptic message. "He wasn't happy, but he said all right; he's tried everything else," she said, hanging up the phone.

Sampson followed her to the kitchen and watched her start to rinse out the glasses. He hurried to the front room, picked up the pillow and blanket, and carried them into the hallway. Off came the telephone receiver to be covered by the pillow, the blanket, and, for good measure, two dusty tomes on Connecticut law. He smiled.

"My, what would Dr. Abel say?" Belinda said with mock seriousness when she saw what he had done. "I mean, after all, that is pretty Freudian."

Oh, fuck Freud, Sampson thought but decided not to say.

73 74 75 76 77 10 9 8 7 6 5 4 3 2 1